Mystic Mustangs
Book 1 - Mystic Mustangs Series

By Candace Rice and Linda Roman

* * * *

Mystic Mustangs Publishing

Prelude

Treading silently across rocks, the young boy's moccasins padded up the mountain trail. Frustration and fear kept his fists tightly clenched during his climb, digging half-moon circles into his palms from his nails. After so many hours, his knuckles seemed frozen and locked in place. The exhaustion and strain seeping through his frail body made him numb. Blinded to the elements and his surroundings, the boy pushed himself forward, focusing solely on his mission. The only pain registering was the welt on his shins which still stung from his father's strikes. He didn't cry... he refused to give in and cry.

Earlier, in the pre-dawn chill before the sun had risen, the boy had been sleeping beneath his warm furs. Through his vivid dreams, he enjoyed a reprieve from the sad truth of his waking life. He envisioned himself as a proud warrior, as tall as any other young boy his age... even taller. And stronger. His bronzed skin shone in the late afternoon sun, reflecting off muscles and shining black hair swaying across his bare back and hips. He sat straight on a paint stallion that had blue eyes, mirroring the sky. A sharp bone knife was thrust through a leather thong on his breeches, and with his bow slung across his back, he led a party of five hunters towards the mountains.

There was a crack of thunder and the dream shattered. The boy bolted upright, wrapped his arms around his shins, and he hugged his skinny legs against his thin chest. The broad silhouetted shadow of his father towering over him, caused a cramping knot in his belly. The young boy stared into his father's dark eyes before dropping a wary glance to the aspen switch clutched in the man's fist. His father's punishment had been swift, and the boy ran a finger along the low single ridge of a swelling, burning welt rising on his shin. Without saying a word, his father turned and left the tepee.

The gray mist of dawn peeked through the tent flap letting the boy know he had overslept again, and he rose quickly to begin his chores. Because he was small for his age, he was given work meant for women and made to rise earlier than the other boys his age. His dreams of being a strong warrior, riding a blue-eyed paint pony and leading tribe hunters, dissolved along with the gray morning mist floating up from the grasses and dissipating from the rising sun.

The boy crossed the grass casting longing gazes at the duns, paints, and bays; all the many beautiful horses his father owned. The fierce man was a proud warrior and held a high position with their tribe, despite producing such a disappointing weakling of a son. A familiar depression spread through the young boy, and as he walked towards the horses his feet moved slower and his shoulders sagged. With his small, frail stature, there seemed no way to earn his father's respect. He could see no herd of fine horses of his own in his future.

The women were already leading their husbands' horses to water, glancing at him and clucking disapproving retorts. Embarrassed that even the women found him lazy and lacking, the boy tried to keep some distance from them while he walked his father's favorite stallion to the stream to drink. It would be the first of nine trips to the water. Nine times the boy would have to suffer the catcalls from the women and the smirks from the tribe's men.

He fought the tears and color rising to his cheeks as a group of boys snickered while they rode their ponies onto the prairie to hunt. Through lowered lashes he blinked rapidly, glancing at the boys with their chests painted in mock warrior signs, bows slapping their long hair in time with the gait of their horses, and the sun illuminating their skin. They had stolen his dream and the boy had nothing left for comfort. He had only the throbbing reminder from his father's switch, dispelling his hope with a painful reminder of his shortcomings.

The stallion lifted its head, balking and pawing the ground at being left behind from the morning run. The hunting party laughed as the boy struggled to hold onto the lead, and in angry frustration he kicked the stallion. The stallion froze and the boy immediately regretted his action, aghast that he should do something so cruel to the beautiful pony. He looked up, deep into the brown almond shaped eyes, seeking forgiveness. Deep inside, stinging his soul far worse than the bruise on his shin, the boy felt shame. The boy lifted his hand and stroked down the soft fur of the white stallion's neck, and he whispered, "I am sorry, iichíile."

The horse's spirit shone through his eyes and he patiently gazed down at boy, reaching inside until the boy understood they shared the same fate. They were both wild, proud spirits, subject to the tribe's rule to survive. Raising his eyes from the boy, the stallion lifted its head and focused its stare towards the mountains. The boy followed its gaze, and his eyes searched beyond the trees and low cliffs. For several moments the two of them stood still, and the boy finally understood what he must do to earn his father's respect.

In an act of defiance and to prove bravery greater than his size, he would dare to enter the Baáhpuuo Isawaxaawuua, the Hitting Rock Mountains. Before he lost his nerve, the boy dropped the stallion's lead and left the water. He ran as swiftly as his young legs would carry him, ignoring the chattering disapproval in the voices of the women.

The stallion whinnied and the boy looked back to see him raised on his strong hind-legs, pawing his front hooves in the air and urging him on. It was true, the young boy was small for his age, but the size of his heart and spirit were another matter. He crossed the rich rolling plains, leaving behind the village where his tribe had gathered.

Now, as he made his way deeper through the tree line, shadows reached out towards him. Frightening dark stretches made his heart pound so hard, it drowned out the sounds of small animals... and perhaps the very thing he feared most. The boy trembled with flashing memories of the legends, spoken in low voices around campfires at night by the elders. The Baáhpuuo were home to the Little People, dwarfs who protected the sacred mountains and their pass through the treacherous cliffs with unmatched ferocity.

Legends passed down through generations had told of them, and the boy's mind whirled with descriptive, frightening stories that had given him nightmares. The shaman spoke of the Little People, standing barely two feet tall, with wide mouths filled with slashing canines and fingers that ended in long sharp claws. The Little People, who used rock arrowheads instead of bone, and annihilated bands of travelers and looted their supplies when they were displeased.

The boy knew he had to offer them a great gift to survive his journey and yet, he had left his home with nothing but the clothes he was wearing. Despite his terror he stood straight, feeling the horse's spirit within him.

For four days he wandered the mountain, climbing higher; fasting and seeking the visions the shamans experienced on their spiritual journeys. The clouds gathered overhead, oppressively covering his view of the clear blue sky. The path became narrower until the walls of the cliffs surrounded him, the ageless rocks leaving him but one path to follow. Higher he climbed, listening to thunder echo off canyon walls. The rain began to fall. Slowly, at first, and then torrents of water muddied the trail, causing him to slip and bruise his hands while he gripped the rock walls. In his mind, he could see the rain flowing down to the prairie far below him… to his tribe and his father… like the tears he refused to cry.

At last he stood at the top of the cliffs, at the very summit of the Baáhpuuo. He was dazed and slightly confused that the trail had ended, and while he looked around, the rain stopped and the clouds parted. The sun burst through and spread its bright golden rays across a high mountain valley, lightening the boy's spirit with a vague sense of wonder. This small burst of pleasure was all he could manage after surviving the journey, as his poor body was worn and bruised and his mind was all but shattered.

Slowly turning and surveying his surroundings, the boy's eyes cleared along with his thoughts when he looked down. The boy stood in awe, gaping at the sight of a herd of beautiful horses whose spirit and wildness flowed across the valley like the wind bending the tall grasses. Certain this must be a vision, the boy trembled in fear that he should witness such a sacred sight. The audacity that one so young and small should receive this gift from the Little People, filled his thoughts with pride and a prick of fear for the tribute they would demand in return.

He gazed out at the horses for a long time, until exhaustion once more clouded his eyes and thoughts and made him wander away. Every part of him ached from his climb, and he crawled under a high ledge, shivering in the cool mountain air. Closing his eyes, he relaxed and drifted into unconsciousness. It was there the Little People found him, starving and near death.

An ancient stared down at the boy. Quizzically at first, and then a smile formed on his face, lifting wrinkles from millennia of time and wisdom. They had been waiting for the messenger from the plains, though for such a grave task, they had expected someone with a more prominent countenance. Instead, they had been given this young boy; battered, bruised, and eyes shadowed with the fear he had fought, to climb to them. The ancient turned to the Little People surrounding him, and they nodded in agreement. There was no more prominent a countenance, than what lived within this boy's spirit.

Many hours later, the boy opened his eyes and a face older than the mountains of the Baáhpuuo stared back at him. He felt his empty stomach clench when the little man spoke. "Why have you come here?" The ancient's eyes narrowed, and once more he studied the pitiful state of the boy. Covered in mud, there were holes worn through the soles of youth's moccasins, showing shadowed purple bruises on his feet from the rocks. The little man lifted his chin and through steel gray eyes he glared down at the prone figure. "You have brought no tribute," he announced.

The boy struggled to sit. Even through his weary state, his fear of the Little People gripped him. Through chattering teeth, he replied, "It is iichíile who has sent me."

The ancient man looked deep into the young Apsáalooke's eyes, and he saw the boy spoke the truth. The horse's spirit *was* joined with his, and there was great sadness. In a low voice, the man said, "You struck out at the stallion."

The boy cringed at the brutal truth of his action, and looking passed his accuser, he noticed the circle of Little People surrounding the ancient. He nodded, silently acknowledging to himself that their punishment would be harsh for such a cruel act, and he prayed for a quick death. Instead, a warm buffalo robe was pulled around him and a bowl of berries and nuts was placed in his lap. Their unexpected kindness surprised him, and when they encouraged him to eat, he scooped fistfuls of food into his mouth.

His fear subsided as his strength returned and he looked more closely at the Little People. It was true, they were small and just over two feet tall, but there the similarity from his tribe's legends ended. Studying and searching for fangs and claws, he could see no indication of them.

They all had piercing gray eyes, sliding to curious smiles as easily as the frightening gaze he had witnessed earlier. Long white hair reached almost to the ground, and they wore leather robes that hung to their ankles. Bright nuts and seeds were stitched into their garments in riotous, colorful designs, and their feet were bare. The ancient in front, the leader, the boy decided, had a feather from the apsaalooke threaded through his hair. This was his tribe's totem and namesake, the fearsome birds with vicious beaks and razor sharp talons. The birds no longer flew through the skies, but the boy recognized the feather as the same feather the shaman of his tribe wore.

The old man smiled at the boy's confusion and the circle of Little People parted. Fear stuck his throat when he saw what had been sitting patiently behind them, just beyond the alcove. The boy looked at a wolf and a cougar, and he wondered if he had been saved only to be sacrificed to the beasts. Other than quietly staring at the sight of him, the beautiful animals remained still. This was truly the magic of the Little People, the boy realized.

The ancient took his hand, and said, "Our protection is that of their proud spirits, joined with ours as iichíile has joined with you." With a gleam of anticipation in his eyes, and in a singsong chant, the old man explained, "We protect the cheéte and iishbíia, as you must now protect the iichíile."

The boy continued to stare uneasily at the predators. They were lean and well-muscled with shining coats and obviously prime, strong animals. "Why would the wolf and cougar need protection?" he asked.

Considering what he discovered to be the true nature of the Little People, the boy doubted these ancients could even protect themselves, much less offer safety to these beasts. Though, it was true this tribe's arrowheads were made of sharp rock, while the Apsaalooke honed theirs of bone. The boy considered the frightening legends and stories he had heard since he was a child, telling how the dwarfs let no one pass through the Baáhpuuo unscathed. He narrowed his gaze on the animals. *Was it their army of wolves and cougars that led the true attack?*

The old man saw realization dawn on the boy. Once more studying the boy's disheveled appearance, the ancient knew well the fortitude and bravery the young Apsaalooke possessed to dare climb to the summit of the Baáhpuuo and risk certain death. The ancient cocked his head, amused with the thought such a young boy was destined to be their ally. He stared into the boy's eyes, acknowledging his small size belied his true strength. "Things are not always as they appear." The ancient turned and nodded towards the wolf and the cougar, and he waved his small arm.

The cougar and wolf stretched. Crackling sounds came from under their fur, and the boy's eyes widened and he crushed himself back into the rock wall. The cougar and wolf blurred, and he rubbed his eyes to clear his vision. *Was their fur really disappearing?* The boy doubted what his eyes were seeing. Fear tightened his throat and his hands began to shake. The cougar and wolf were unfolding, becoming straighter, until before him stood two white people. A proud dark haired man and a woman with a golden mane gazed silently back at him.

The old man turned, and seeing the disbelief in the boy's eyes, he chuckled. "Our magic is strong."

It took a long time for the boy to speak. "What is the purpose?" His mouth was so dry he could barely get the words out. These were the white people he had heard of and avoided, though he had never seen. His questioning voice quivered, "Do all of the white people possess your magic?" The thought of this made him nervous. It had been many lifetimes since the apsaalooke had flown in the sky, and long before the white man had invaded their lands. These new people had never seen the bird, so they named his tribe Crow… and the boy wondered if it was an omen.

"No, these shifters came from a white tribe that dared to pass through the Baáhpuuo without paying homage." A distasteful, angry expression crossed over the ancient's features. "Their hunters took advantage of our elk and bear, leaving carcasses of half-eaten meat in their wake. The travelers' horses were taxed, pulling heavily overloaded wagons of useless trinkets up the mountain, and being beaten when they fell or stumbled."

The boy was surprised to see tears swimming in the gray gazes of the ancients watching him. He imagined the horses, fighting the same rocks that had bruised his

13

own feet, pushed beyond limits and struggling with heavy loads. He envisioned striped lashes on thin rumps and flanks from whips, and tender mouths from where men yanked on bridals to force the overburdened animals across uneven trails through the mountains. The cruelty of such a scene made the boy shudder, and he realized the Little People were sharing their vision of the actual white man's passage unfolding.

In a soft voice, the old man continued. "At night, we sent the cheéte and iishbíia to gather around the dying animals and offer them solace before they journeyed home. Our beasts meant no harm, and yet the white people shot and killed them." Deep sadness filled his eyes, and his hand rubbed his chest with the memory of their guilt for sending the cheéte and iishbíia into slaughter. It was a heavy weight on the mystics' spirits. They had meant for the strong beasts to comfort the iichíile, and instead they were killed and sent on their own final journey.

The little man turned towards his creations, and his expression softened. "These two fought to stop the massacre, and so they escaped the fate of the others." He remembered their ferocity in fighting their friends. The man had managed to disarm two of the shooters, and the woman set fire to one of the wagons as a distraction. She had cradled the head of a cougar in her lap, using damp lace from her petticoat to clean blood off its fur, long after the amber eyes had glazed over.

The ancients could see that this man and woman did not share the same spirit as the murderers. The old man took the young boy's hand and gazed into his eyes. The gray in the ancient's stare had dulled, and his eyes were edged in weariness. "Like you, these white people were called to join with the spirit of the wolf and cougar they had seen slayed."

The boy considered his words, and he shivered at the memory of kicking the stallion. "Then, I am to become a horse?" Summoning his courage, the small boy raised his head proudly and decided the sentence was fair.

The ancient laughed and shook his head. "Oh no, little warrior." He stroked through the boy's dusty black hair, and the boy felt a surge of something unexplainable yet completely fulfilling wash through him. His strength was completely returned, and his mind and eyes were sharp and clear. The mystic issued his edict. "You are to keep the secret of the Baáhpuuo cheéte and iishbíia, and they are to protect the iichíile."

The man sighed in a deep weary breath, shaking his head and allowing his long white hair to sweep the ground. The ancient spoke in a voice that was almost a whisper, and filled with so much sorrow the boy could feel the mystic's pain. "Our time of magic is passing. In our visions, we see the horses hunted down, killed for their meat and brutalized with misunderstanding."

The ancient closed his eyes, wishing this premonition were not true. Opening them again, he turned from the boy and in his shambling gait he walked over to the form-shifters. "The cheéte and iishbíia can do something the Apsaalooke cannot, for we have seen your proud people will carry the burden of their own unjust challenges." He looked up at the man and woman, and said, "They can walk among the white people and save the iichíile, but to do this, their secret spirit must be kept safe by your tribe."

The boy stared at the ancient, and then to the silent man and woman. His brows knit together and after some thought, he asked, "How are we to protect them? If they walk among the white tribes and the Apsaalooke do not... I don't understand." The admission of his ignorance made him tremble, and he wondered if the ancient would reconsider and decide to kill him, instead.

The ancient ran his hand through the woman's blond hair and she smiled down at him. "The cheéte and iishbíia will always long to return to the mountains, where they can shift at will and run free. The Apsaalooke will make their home near the Baáhpuuo, guarding the sunrise side of the mountains so the shifters can enjoy the land." The relief in the shifters' eyes shined down at the ancient. They were vulnerable and still adjusting to their new status, and the Little People had seen to their needs. If the ancients made a pact with the tribe to protect them, the shifters would fulfill their task and save the wild horses.

The ancient walked back to the boy, leaned forward, and reached his small hand to the boy's chest. Placing his palm over his heart, he said, "I will teach you the healing magic. It is a powerful medicine and when applied quickly, it will cure the cheéte and iishbíia from serious wounds."

The old man stared into the boy's eyes. "The Apsaalooke will protect the shifters when they are in their animal form, so the wolf and cougar can share their spirit with the land. Your tribe holds this spirit for the mountains and plains, the rivers and lakes, in their heart. Together, the Apsaalooke, the cheéte, and the iishbíia, will be a circle of protection for the iichíile."

The man's eyes turned silver, and the boy felt his gaze penetrate deep into his mind in warning. "This circle must never be broken, or the spirit of the Baáhpuuo will die and the iichíile will disappear.

The heavy weight of anguish crushed the boy's chest. The thought of a land without the beautiful horses was unimaginable, and the boy realized the honorable task the Apsaalooke had been given. He spent three more days with the Little People, walking among the spelled cheéte and iishbíia. They spoke quietly with him, swearing their loyalty to the iichíile, and the boy knew their white spirit had melded with that of their beast. The woman cried and buried her head into the man's chest, when she shared the story of the horrendous killing surrounding their wagons. In hushed fearful voices, they spoke of white travelers crossing the passage, and how they now hid to avoid them.

The boy began to understand their fear. Whether in animal or human form, they would be feared if their secret were known. Others from the white people tribe would hunt them down and kill them, just as their band of travelers had hunted and killed the beasts surrounding their wagons. The shape shifters would do as the Little People requested and protect the iichíile. In return, they trusted the boy to have the Apsaalooke keep their secret, and to honor the circle of protection.

The boy pledged loyalty to the Little People's sacred treaty before he traveled back down the mountain. He returned to his tribe no longer a boy, but as a tall, strong man. At last, his father stood proud while presenting his son to the tribe. As they listened to his story, no one doubted his vision and they made him a leader. They would follow the Little Peoples' edict, protecting the secret of the shape shifters and in this way the Apsaalooke would also protect their beloved mustangs.

Centuries passed, and to the white man, the name Apsaalooke was forgotten. The tribe became known as Crow. The Baáhpuuo Isawaxaawuua was renamed after a white warrior and drawn on the maps as the Pryor Mountains. Regardless of these changes, the tribe and form-shifters fought hard, and the Baáhpuuo were now home to the largest mustang preserve in the country.

There were almost forty thousand acres of rolling hills, pastures, and wetlands for the iichíile to run wild and free. The land was protected by laws and agreements with the BLM; the Bureau of Land Management. The policies were initiated, fought for, and enforced by the rigorous efforts of the cheéte and iishbíia. The Crow Nation overlapped the Baáhpuuo on one side… and they kept a vigilant, silent, watchful eye on it all.

As the years passed, more and more often, the werewolves and werecats were leaving the mountains. Other herds of feral horses were facing inhumane roundups and despicable slaughter. The shape shifters formed rescue leagues, holding the BLM accountable and establishing small ranch sanctuaries for the mustangs.

It was difficult for the cheéte and iishbíia to remain off the mountain. Visions of their ancestors' freedom and running in were-shape shifted form, filled their dreams and called them home. They fought the feral instincts of their animal spirits, and their maddening desire to join the iichíile on the foothills, grasslands, and plains.

Chapter I

Panic and fear raced through the terrified young woman's mind as she ran; chest heaving and dragging breath hissed through her lips. The shadows from the dark foliage of the aspens and pines blocked her view and she couldn't see the sides of the mountain trail. The dense coverage of tree leaves kept the night air cold and damp; too wet and too heavy. She couldn't get a deep breath and her lungs begged to be filled with air.

Behind her, she heard the flat sounds of his boots landing on dirt and rock and following at a steadily consistent pace. No matter how fast she ran he was gaining on her, and there was nowhere for her to hide. All she could do was follow the narrow trail up the mountain, travelling forward. She was confused and sensed a feeling of loss; she knew she was leaving someone behind. She could not remember who or why, and it scared her. All she knew was that she had to go on, push her exhaustion aside and move up the trail... get away.

Far behind her on the plain she heard the distant thunder of horses' hooves. She ran on, up, and still further up the *mountain until the trees thinned. On her left loomed a solid rock wall, and to the right was a sight that chilled her. A cliff fell away into blackness, and she felt herself drawn close to the edge.*

The rumble of the galloping horses seemed louder, and she pictured the herd funneling to single file between the trees marking the beginning of the ascent. The sound distracted her from the pull from the ledge, a moment before she stepped off. She trembled as she watched scattered pebbles roll over the edge, clattering off the side until they landed at the bottom of the ravine.

Ahead, she heard a wolf's wailing cry into the starlit sky. It was answered by a deeper howl from behind her on the path, obscuring the sound of the man chasing her. The gut-wrenching call of the wolves did not frighten her. Instead, they seemed to pull her nervously forward, simultaneously emptying her soul and filling it with mourning for the past.

The trail ended abruptly, opening to a large clearing with a dirt tract weaving through patches of grass. She looked to the left, to a wall of rocks and caves. In the middle of the open space, a small fire glowed. Bursts of lit ash floated into the sky above the flame, and within the circle of its golden illumination, she saw a small wolf. It sat facing away from her and she stopped, trapped.

The footsteps behind her slowed to a walk and she flinched when a hand rested on her shoulder. It held firmly, keeping her in place while lips brushed her ear. "It's alright. You're alright, now." His whispered words sent a chill of want and dread through her.

She turned and tilted her head to look up at the man. He was tall, with long wavy dark hair and gray-blue eyes reflecting the light of the fire. The man was smiling at her, and with his hand still on her shoulder, he guided her towards one of the caves.

The opening faced the fire, washing the cavern walls with dim light. Blankets were strewn across the dirt floor and she felt brimming tears when she looked up into the man's shadowed face. "I can't do this. I can't be here," she argued, still confused and feeling she left something behind. The incessant clamoring of hooves was so near now, she could hear the individual sounds of the horses snorting and whinnying as they charged ever closer.

She drew back against the cool cavern wall and he stepped closer, embracing her with one arm and holding her still. "Calm down, you're alright," he repeated. His deep voice floated passed her fear and uncertainty. "This is where you're meant to be." He leaned down, and she was shadowed by the brim of his black hat when he kissed her.

Despite the unusual situation, she was disoriented by a calmness filling her, and she realized her panic and fearful dread were subsiding. A part of her sensed the man holding her felt right, and her feelings of loss were going away. Slowly, her arms reached up around his neck and her fingers trailed through his silky hair.

Stroking gently down her back, the man felt her relax and surrender. He guided them down onto the blankets and caressed her cheek with his thumb. Staring into her eyes, he murmured, "I didn't know you would be so beautiful."

Outside the cavern the horses charged into the clearing. A stallion reared, pawing the air in a victorious dance. His long mane and tail whipped in the breeze, silhouetted by the flames of the wolf's fire.

Lexi woke up sweating in a tangle of sheets. The dream …or perhaps it was a nightmare… was always the same. Every night for the past two weeks, she had awoken anxious and confused with her heart pounding so hard, she could feel it through her chest wall when she laid her palm over it. Blinking wide eyes in the darkness, the red numbers on the clock showed her it was the same time, 2 am, and she turned on the bedside lamp. Lexi picked up the journal and the pen she left on the nightstand and waited for her hand to stop trembling. Staring at the blank page, she chewed on the end of the pen in thought, preparing to write down what little she could remember. By morning, even that faint memory would be gone.

She wrote furiously, scrawling sweeping thoughts across the page until the fleeting dream finally dissolved and she could not recall anything else. She tried to pry open heavy doors to blanketed memories and finally reached only darkness. There was more, she was certain of it. But the elusive thoughts could not be grasped, so Lexi closed the journal and turned off the light. It was a long time before she was able to sleep.

When she opened her eyes, she could tell by the sunlight washing across her bedroom that she had overslept again. Eyeing the journal nervously, Lexi re-read the short passage she wrote the night before, and then she tugged on her clothes and hurried to the kitchen.

"Girl, you look like something rode hard and put away wet." The tanned, weathered face of her father smiled at Lexi from across the kitchen table. His long gray hair was in its usual shaggy disarray, waiting to be squashed under his old cowboy hat. Lexi walked to the counter and missed a step, when he asked, "The dream again?"

She poured herself a cup of coffee, feeling slightly guilty she had not gotten up early enough to make the pot. "Dad, I wrote some of it down last night." Her eyes narrowed in concentration while she stared into her coffee. "It's so weird. I mean, now that I see the words, I remember the part I wrote. But nothing before or after, if there is anything." She looked over at her father and shrugged. "I think maybe that's when I wake up."

"Wanna' talk about it, or is it one of those 'Michelle only' discussions?" Jacob leaned back and took a sip of what Lexi discovered was very potent brew.

She frowned and pursed her lips around a mouthful of coffee, managed to swallow, and asked, "Gosh Dad, how many scoops did you use? I need a knife and fork to cut through this." Lexi braced herself and took another sip. Sometimes she wondered if he made it so badly just to encourage her to get to the kitchen before him. The color rose in her cheeks at his suggestion her dream might be a 'girl-talk only' discussion, and she tried to ignore the fact that he had figured that it must involve a man. "I'm running up a path on a mountain with a guy chasing me. When we get to the top, there's a fire with a wolf sitting near it." Lexi shrugged and offered an evasive reply in an attempt to sound indifferent. "I guess I figure out the man is someone I should know, because I end up not being afraid of him."

Jacob rocked forward, feeling a haunting panic while he studied her. There were shadows circling beneath her eyes, and his thoughts flew to his wife, Vanessa. With Lexi's long, thick auburn hair and indigo flecks shot through her gray eyes; the full lips and high cheekbones… Jacob sighed. Lexi looked so much like her mother it made his heart ache, sometimes. "Where do you think you are in this dream? We're in Florida and I haven't taken you to the mountains since your mom was with us. Do you recognize any of it?"

Her father's gray eyes were unusually bright, and the intensity of his stare seemed odd to her. "No idea." Lexi had vague memories of camping when she was young. It was so long ago, and she could only capture small bits of the time spent with her mother. "Maybe I'll go through some of the old photos tonight and see if anything looks familiar. It would be great if this is just some crazy fantasy about a place we used to camp. The dream seems so real, though." Lexi put her cup in the sink, giving up on the sludge.

Jacob shook off the depressing thoughts of Vanessa. Those remembrances consumed enough of his time when he was working on tack… or at night when he climbed into bed alone. "Well, it wouldn't surprise me if it's 'cause of the way you got that room of yours fixed up." He scowled and his thick wiry brows knit together. "Why you couldn't have gotten fixed on horses, I'll never figure out." Jacob made no secret he was uneasy with her wolf obsession. Her walls were covered with posters of them and she must have fifty little statues stashed on every surface. He tipped his cup at her and added, "It amazes me those pictures didn't give you nightmares long before this."

"I see enough of the horses all day, Dad. You know I've always had a thing about wolves. I don't know, I guess they're like my totem. This morning I looked at the posters, and none of the cliffs in them match my dream. I think it's something else." Lexi plopped down in the railed chair across from him and pulled on her worn boots.

"After you feed the horses, McMillan wants you to call." Jacob smiled and waited for his daughter's reaction.

"Don't tell me. He wants to get rid of Brutus again." Lexi laughed, the dream temporarily forgotten, and she rose and put her hands on her hips. "What did he do this time?"

"Broke through the fence to get to that fancy new mustang mare. The mare's so wild she kicked the hell out of the old stud and almost gelded him." Jacob was laughing now, as well. At least once a week, Mac called him with some frustrating crime his favorite stallion had perpetrated. Sometimes it was kicking through planks in his stall, other times it was balking at having his hooves trimmed.

"Seems like the poor guy paid for his visit in spades. I'll calm Mac down when I finish feeding and working with the horses. We both know he'll never really get rid of that old guy." Lexi grabbed a muffin and headed to the door to start her chores.

She stepped off the porch, looked across the pasture, and smiled. Their twenty-year-old double-wide mobile home, sat pretty much in the middle of the ten acre mini-ranch she shared with her dad. On the fence-line stood a small barn with a tack room and three sturdy corrals were on the right.

Lexi loved the corrals and she remembered back to when each one had been built. She smiled and thought about how hard she had campaigned for that last one… the nine footer… the *mustang* corral. So far, they hadn't jumped out of *that*. She sighed. Lexi had lived here almost all her life and she still loved the place.

Parked by the porch, their faded red pick-up truck rested under the branches of an oak. It was old, but Jacob kept it carefully maintained. Between the barn and the house, the horse trailer sat with the back ramp opened and laying in the grass. It could carry as many as six horses back and forth to the monthly auctions and was most expensive thing they owned. Sunchaser Ranch was painted proudly across the back and down the sides.

It was Friday, and Lexi figured she could get the current five auction horses out for one last ride before they were loaded up to sell early the next morning. Her dad was a whiz at picking which untrained horses they'd buy. After they brought them home, it was Lexi's job to work with them so they could be sold at the next auction.

Jacob made money on the sale of rideable, well trained, and well-mannered horses. Lexi made a percentage for both starting and finishing the horses, and then riding them in the ring. Other owners had her ride for them because the horses always brought more money when the pretty girl easily put them through their paces before prospective buyers. She also did private training on the side for people and gave riding lessons.

When Lexi graduated, there was a brief mention of college while they stood outside the high school gym. With cheerful commotion surrounding them, Lexi and Jacob stood still in an awkward silence. Their short conversation consisted of two uncomfortably spoken sentences.

Jacob looked down at his dusty boots. "Lexi, I got some money saved if you want to go to college."

"No, I don't think so, Dad," she replied, looking down at the toes of her own worn boots sticking out from under her graduation gown. They never spoke of it again, even when her best friend, Michelle, left for school in Gainesville. She missed Michelle's company, but the thought of not being around the mustangs was too depressing.

Lexi inhaled the warm air and raised her head to the sun before crossing the yard to a small paddock. She smiled and climbed over the pipe railing. Standing completely relaxed and holding out her hand, she watched the nervous three-year old mustang. Lexi had been working with the filly everyday now, first driving it around at a walk or trot, until finally, after many patient hours, the filly joined up. Even now, after almost nine weeks, the filly stood halfway out of the stall door, trying to decide if she trusted Lexi enough to walk forward.

"Come on Daisy-May. Come on, sweet thing," Lexi crooned softly. The mustang rescuers had brought her to the ranch two months ago. The half-starved horse had put on enough weight so her ribs could no longer be counted, however the scars from where the halter had grown into her nose and the sides of her face would always be a tragic reminder of the abuse she had suffered. Lexi had cried when the Vet had cut the halter off, peeling fur and skin with it.

The man who had won the bid at the wild horse and burro auction and adopted the mustang, was up on charges for animal cruelty. His impulsive two hundred dollar purchase for his daughter's newest infatuation was going to cost him thousands and probably jail time. Lexi considered turnabout fair play, and she wished they would tighten a strap across his face and let him starve for a while. Not very charitable, but she was always on the horses' side.

Over the years, she had patiently tamed many of the traumatized horses. Sometimes she could almost feel their panic and fear. She had read every book at the library she could get her hands on about mustangs, though there weren't very many.

When Michelle's folks bought her a laptop for college, she gave Lexi her desktop computer. It opened a whole new world of information for her. With only a landline the connections were slow, but Lexi patiently waited for sites about mustangs to load, and she read every article on the internet she could find about them. Michelle shared her obsession, and they would angrily read over the accounts of the mustang roundups.

First, the beautiful feral horses were frightened by the loud chopping sounds of helicopters, chasing them down from the mountains and the only home they had ever known... the BLM lands out west... lands where they were able to play, breed, and run wild. Then, the wranglers took over. Strange man-beasts the mustangs did not recognize, waving hats, yelping, and twirling lassos like flying snakes.

The horses were rounded up, roped, thrown down, pushed into corrals and forced into chutes to be branded. After the terrifying roundup was over, the mustangs were dragged into trailers or sent by train to a life in captivity. The fear caused some to withdraw and spiral into depression. Others panicked in the confining quarters, while the familiar scent and sight of their homeland disappeared along with their freedom.

According to the BLM rhetoric, the sanctioned lands were overgrazed through overpopulated herds, and the auction adoptions were meant to provide a humane existence and home for the animals. Even with a rigid application, including a drawn map of the acceptable lodging for the horse, some made their way to slaughterhouses… and some made their way to places like Harry Timbleton's fancy ranch estate.

The horse had been quickly forgotten when his daughter could not catch her to ride the day after she arrived at Timbleton's ranch. With a shrug of her shoulders, Harry's daughter took off in her other Mustang, a cherry red convertible. Two months later, an anonymous neighbor called the SPCA. They found auction horse 4805 barely able to stand, with glazed eyes from the pain of the ingrown leather halter. No one had even bothered to name her.

"Come on, Daisy-May. That's a good girl. That's my brave girl." Lexi stopped talking. She only greeted the nervous animals when she arrived at the paddock so they were aware of her presence. After that, it was all in her actions and movements, and she cleared her mind to speak the body language the wild horse understood.

Lexi began to walk slowly away from the horse and around the fence line. Even though she focused on her breathing and rhythm, the horse took a step back into the safety of the stall as she walked closer. Lexi continued walking slow, not even looking at Daisy-May as she passed, still keeping her body relaxed. Straightening raised the energy, like an invisible force of warning, and this horse would respond with nervous agitation. It would be a while before Daisy-May felt safe enough for Lexi to use any energy as communication.

For now, she walked around the paddock with her shoulders slumped and knees loose, mostly studying the worn path her boots left in the dirt. On her second pass, Lexi felt a nervous soft nudge against her shoulder, but she kept her eyes focused down or straight ahead. *That's a good girl. That's my brave girl.*

Daisy-May did not have an aggressive personality. She was only frightened and looking for a leader. In the wild, this would be the alpha mare, and she would be part of her herd. Here, it would be Lexi, calming the horse with her predictable, non-threatening movements and making the mustang feel safe.

After two more circuits she stopped in front of the stall with the horse standing behind her. Lexi remained in her relaxed repose, giving the horse time to 'lick and chew' as she considered trusting this stranger. With slow, deliberate movements, Lexi reached over her shoulder. In a few moments, warm breath caressed her knuckles, investigating her human scent. It was a scent that had accompanied danger and pain, but the horse desperately wanted to trust something in this frightening new world.

Smiling at the ground, Lexi reached her fingers out, holding them together so they would not touch the soft skin of the horse's nose like claws. She stroked down Daisy-May's muzzle and slowly turned. Leaning her head close to the horse, they matched breath for a few moments.

Her hand stroked down the brown neck and over the cryptic BLM freeze identification brand, until she gently rubbed her withers. Lexi had been in the paddock for half an hour, coaxing the horse to accept her touch. She had done this twice a day for the past week. Today would be a tough one for both of them. Lexi glanced into the liquid brown almond shaped eyes, looking for trust.

She reached for the rope halter she had looped through her belt. Harry Timbleton's torture device was leather, and she did not want to frighten Daisy-May with that scent. She waited until the mustang nuzzled and sniffed the straps, watching until the tension released from her wary stance. When her head dropped down and a big blowout came from her nose, Lexi gently trailed the rope halter across her cheeks and over her neck. At the first sign of fear, Lexi retreated, taking the halter away, and then re-approaching. It took another half an hour to get it buckled, and both the horse and girl sagged in relief.

The bright blue halter was loose enough not to hurt her, yet it would not flop around or catch on anything. *Oh, my brave girl. Good girl, Daisy-May.* It had been an anxious experience for both of them, with the horse learning to accept, and Lexi keeping her calm with her vigilant, easy movements. This small victory would be the turning point in her training. The halter represented Daisy-May's greatest fear and pain, and she had placed her trust in Lexi's calm, knowledgeable leadership.

The horse followed her into the stall, and Lexi scooped her feed into the bucket and filled her water. There was hay left in the hanging net bag from the night feeding. She ran her hand down the mustang's back and flanks, feeling good about the progress the two of them made. With a 'thank you' to Daisy-May, Lexi left the barn to work with the regular auction stock.

Chapter II

The rest of the morning, Lexi played with the horses in the round pen, desensitizing, circling, side-stepping, backing, and teaching patterns; all of this prepared them for riding. When she was certain they were responding to her, she saddled them and rode them in the pasture. She took them through an obstacle course of ramps, waving strips tied to the branches of trees, and walking them either passed or over a frightening sheet of black plastic, crumpled and secured to the ground. At the end of any given month, when she finished with the training, the horses had overcome their fears and become accustomed to unusual obstructions.

One pretty black gelding had the makings of a good barrel racer, so she had been spending the last week working him around the large plastic drums in the shamrock pattern. For competition he would need more training, but Lexi decided she would run the barrels in the ring tomorrow in case a starry-eyed cowgirl recognized his potential.

"He looks pretty good, Lexi," Jacob called out. "Hopefully, we'll have the right crowd for him." Jacob was squinting at the horse, mentally judging the gelding's worth. The truck needed new tires.

"Yeah, Dad. His legs are strong and he's surefooted enough, but he's not as tight around the turns as I'd like." Lexi dismounted and started walking the horse before offering it water.

Jacob strolled beside her and he glanced towards the paddock where the mustang stood grazing. His eyes narrowed and he smiled, nodding his head. "You got a halter on her. Good. I wasn't sure you'd get through to her." Sometimes it worked out that way, and the best they could do was find an adoptive home that understood the horse could only be left in the pasture. Either due to their feral instincts, or terrifying experiences since their capture that had left them scarred, they would never be tame.

Jacob reached for the reins. "Here, I'll take him. Michelle wants you to call her." Jacob watched Lexi walk towards the house. Her auburn braid swung across her back, just as it had when she was a little girl. The slender waist and long legs didn't match that memory of her though, and it didn't seem fair. Time had passed too quickly, and he realized Lexi was pretty much grown up now.

Along with the melancholy of the passing years, he felt an internal warning. *Damn dream.* Jacob watched Lexi walk into the house, and he led the gelding to the water trough. He sure as hell did not want her asking too many questions. And he certainly did not want her finding any photos she might recognize. *She had been so little, would she even remember the place if she did see it?* He frowned.

Earlier this morning, Jacob had quickly shuffled through all the photographs he could find while Lexi had been working the horses. He had taken out seven of them and hidden them in the hidey-hole in his closet, where he kept the leather-bound book that held the secrets of his past. He was sure there were more pictures, but he had searched everyplace he could think of and came up empty-handed.

Lexi called Mac and he had already calmed down about his stallion. "That little mustang kicked him hard and left a pretty good mark on his hip, but he's walking okay and it doesn't look like it will scar. Damn old fool shoulda' known better than to mess with her," Mac grumbled.

"Do you need help fixing the fence?" Lexi offered.

"Nah, I fixed it this morning and the mustang calmed down when I locked Brutus in his stall."

"Okay, then.   Are you going to the auction tomorrow?" Lexi asked.

Mac snorted.   "You'll probably see Brutus loaded up.   I've had just about enough of his antics.   They always set me up for extra work."

Lexi smiled.   "Well, I guess we'll see you there. Call if he gives you anymore trouble."

"Will do," Mac replied.   "See you in the morning."

With her call to McMillan out of the way, Lexi dialed Michelle's number. "Hey girl, what's up?" Lexi cradled the phone on her shoulder while she poured some sweet tea.

"Honestly, Lexi. Why don't you get a cell phone? You are like the *only* person in the world who doesn't have one." Michelle issued the same familiar argument and she expected the same familiar reply.

"Waste of money," Lexi replied.   "You know what happens with your phone out here. We're in a dead area and I can't even get DSL for the computer." Secretly, Lexi didn't want to get tied down like she had seen others do. They were constantly answering music blasts or tapping frantically moving fingers for text messaging, even in the movies. "You want to go riding?"

Michelle chewed her lip a moment, and asked suspiciously, "Are you done for the day?" She *so* did not want to get stuck helping Lexi wash and groom all the horses for the auction. She had made that mistake before.

"I've got a couple hours before they need to be cleaned up. Let me grab a sandwich and I'll head over to your place." The girls ended their quick talk and Lexi made lunch for her dad and herself.

After she finished, she saddled up Travis and headed over to Michelle's larger ranch a mile away. Travis spread into a gentle canter, stretching his legs while Lexi enjoyed the gentle breeze. She slowed him to a walk for the last quarter mile. She had been training the young buckskin for a ten-year-old girl who needed a gentle pleasure horse.

Michelle's folks owned five hundred acres of more than decent pastureland. They ran cows and beautiful quarter horses. White polymer fencing surrounded the grazing horses, with well-maintained stables and outbuildings. They had a huge two story house, landscaped yards, and a swimming pool out back. Luckily, Michelle's parents liked Lexi and allowed her friendship with their daughter, despite the apparent discrepancy in social standing. Neighbors were good distances apart out here, and the girls had been friends since they met in kindergarten.

After high school, Michelle had left for college in Gainesville, yet she drove home almost every weekend, choosing to miss the usual campus parties and distractions. With summer a few months away, Michelle had decided she was going to take this summer off and return to school for the fall semester. It would be exciting to take a real vacation, one without her folks. She had mentioned it to Lexi the last time she was home, and they agreed to start saving to go someplace special.

Michelle trotted up on Midnight Blue, with her golden-blonde ponytail swinging behind her. Her exotic green eyes flashed a smile, and Lexi had a memory from Halloween, when they were young. Every year, Michelle's mom gave in and used eyeliner to streak whiskers across her cheeks, because she insisted on being a cat. Just once, Peggy wished her beautiful daughter would be a princess.

Michelle reined to a stop beside her. "How do the horses look?" she asked. Even though Michelle had plenty of other friends, like Jenny and Anne, they usually stayed at college for the weekend parties, so when Lexi had her auction weekend Michelle was at loose ends.

"Pretty good, one might go for a barrel horse. Definite potential." Lexi felt kind of silly saying that with the superior bred horses grazing in a pasture beside her.

"And Daisy-May?"

Lexi smiled, thinking of her well-earned triumph. She had been truly worried Daisy-May might not be able to break out of her panic. "I got a halter on her this morning, so I should be able to start her on groundwork by the end of the week. They usually snap out of it pretty quickly once they deal with their trauma."

"The rescuers have approved two of the permanent places I found for her." Michelle had better connections to find the abused horses homes, and after her careful instructions, they always passed BLM requirements.

Her concern for the mustangs was as genuine as Lexi's, and Michelle made sure the new prospective owners judiciously followed their agreement. Ultimately, the girls chose the new owner by mostly an internal, instinctive feeling as to who projected the right demeanor and personality to work with the horse's trauma and would be the best match for a particular mustang.

"Is one of them Amy Johnson?" Lexi considered the quiet girl. Even at her young age, she had a calm determination and heartfelt compassion for Daisy-May.

"Yes. They were a little worried because she's only sixteen, but when they checked out the facilities and her record with FFA at school, it helped. And her parents are totally behind it."

"Out of the prospects I've met, I think she's the best match. Amy has a soft voice and I think she'll have the patience to work with Daisy-May."

Michelle nodded. "Well that, and she cried almost as hard as you did when we left your place. She couldn't believe anyone could be so cruel to a horse." Michelle reached down and stroked her mare's neck. "You're still saving for vacation, right?"

"Yep, but I haven't mentioned it to Dad yet. If we're only gone a couple weeks, I might be able to at least green break a couple before he has to turn them around for sale. Any idea where we should go?" Lexi hadn't really left the area for years, except for the twenty-five mile trip to the auction.

"Not yet. I'm looking at a few places, but we'll decide when I'm done with school." From her saddle, Michelle reached down and opened the latch on the gate to the bigger cow pasture. The two girls made it through the gate and Lexi leaned over to slide the bar back through the posts.

Now that they were a distance from the house and riding in what they considered to be their private territory, Michelle fired off questions. "Now, what's going on? You've got circles under your eyes. You're not getting sick are you?"

"No, at least I don't think so." Lexi plucked at a fraying stitch on her saddle horn. "I'm still having that weird dream I told you about last week," she admitted.

Michelle stared at a calf jumping around its mother and nodded her head. "You didn't tell me anything about it, though. You said you couldn't remember."

Michelle took two bottles of water out of her saddle pack and tossed one to Lexi.

"Last night, I wrote a part in my journal when I woke up. I read it this morning." Lexi relayed the story of the mysterious man. "I'm going through some pictures tonight to see if anything looks familiar. Dad and Mom used to take me camping in the mountains when I was little, so maybe it's some sort of memory."

"Could be, but why now? I mean, your mom's been gone fifteen years." Michelle did not like reminding Lexi of her mother's abandonment and never mentioned her unless Lexi did first.

"I don't know." Lexi's fingers left the saddle horn and she picked nervously at the lip of her water bottle. For some reason, whenever she was around Michelle, it seemed more important to figure out the meaning of her dream. "None of it makes sense. This isn't any kind of anniversary of her leaving or anything. Dad says she took off in July." Lexi followed Michelle's gaze across the waving grasses at a herd of cattle. "I'm sure it's the same dream every night, so it's gotta' mean something, don't you think?" It was confusing trying to link the dream to an unknown event, as well as an unknown location, with an unknown... well, she wasn't ready to admit what *he* was.

"Did your dad have any thoughts about it?" Michelle combed her fingers absently through her horse's dark mane. Lexi's strange dream nagged at her, but she didn't know why.

"Not a clue. He's the one that got me thinking about going through the photos, though." Lexi turned her horse's head in lateral flexion. "Travis, stop that." He had managed to crowd Michelle's valuable quarter horse, and then tried to nip her.

"Well, I know I'm going to regret this, but how about some company? I'll help you sort through the pictures and spend the night. Maybe I can wake you up at a different part of the dream and we can piece together more of it. I haven't been to the auction in a while, so it might be fun." Michelle tried to sound enthusiastic. She had not gone to an auction with Lexi for over a year. It was mostly a long, hot, sweaty, dusty day.

Lexi laughed and offered to let her off the hook. "You don't have to do that, Michelle. I know you hate it. I'd love to have you spend the night, though."

"No, really. Jenny and Anne are the only two we used to hang around with who still come back here once in a while, and they decided to stay at school this weekend. It's either go with you or be bored and stuck working here. Let's ride back and I'll pack." Michelle turned her horse and Lexi knew this meant the matter was settled.

After the dinner dishes were washed and the horses were taken care of, the girls sat on the living room floor with shoe boxes stuffed with pictures. Jacob had always been a camera buff and he still took pictures of Lexi, but neither of them had the patience or desire to put them in scrapbooks. Six boxes stuffed with photos were stacked around the girls, and they each reached for a carton to sift through. They quickly pushed several to the side, because they were obviously filled with pictures taken after Jacob and Lexi moved to Florida. They only needed to go through the boxes of photos with the mountains.

Jacob sat sitting in his old recliner watching television. Lexi held up pictures, discussing when and where certain events took place and smiling at the memories. These were the boxes of photos from the mountains when Lexi was a little girl that Jacob had pawed through earlier in the day. He was reasonably optimistic he had removed anything questionable, and then Lexi surprised him.

"Hold on." She dashed to her room and came out with another small box of pictures.

Jacob's eyes widened. He had missed this one. Michelle heard a growling noise and glanced over at Lexi's dad. For an instant, she thought she saw a flash of something strange pass over his features, but she shrugged it off when Lexi sat down beside her.

They sifted through her private collection. She had already separated a lot of the pictures taken when she was young, and the pictures of her mom were placed in their own pile. *Vanessa.* Lexi smiled to herself as faint vague memories of her mother's soft voice filled her thoughts. There were never any words... just gentle murmurs she struggled to make out. Lexi thought of her mom as a phantom in her life, and her dad rarely spoke of her. Concentrating on the pictures, Lexi missed the look of distress that passed over her father's face.

Jacob had had a feeling that some of the pictures of Vanessa were missing from his earlier search, but he had been hurrying through them and hadn't been sure. He pretended to watch the television while glancing down at Lexi. It had not occurred to him that she kept a separate stash of photos, and he had the uneasy feeling that fifteen years trying to protect her was about to come to an end.

Lexi handed Michelle a picture of her taken when she was about four years old. Behind Lexi stood a much younger Jacob, smiling at a pretty young woman. A tent with a campfire was in the background, with a lake and mountains in the distance.

"Dad used to have great camera gear." She twisted around and looked up at her father. "Remember the tripod and how you'd run to make it in the picture before the timer went off?" She turned back towards Michelle. "He'd be all out of breath after running back to us, and try to pretend he'd just been standing there with us all along." Lexi laughed while her friend studied the picture. "Of course, now he has one of those fancy digital things."

Michelle looked at the picture, running a finger over the surface while her mouth dropped open and her eyes widened. She had never seen a picture of Lexi's mom before. "Jeeze, Lexi. You look just like her." Michelle glanced between the picture and her friend. She looked up at Jacob, and she thought how hard it must have been to have his missing wife's double in the house as a constant reminder.

Jacob leaned down to look at the picture, reading her thoughts. "Lexi does look a lot like her mother." He looked fondly at Lexi, and he saw Vanessa's big gray-blue eyes and wide smile in his daughter's face. "Vanessa wasn't quite as tall. They have the same eyes and auburn hair, though." He rested back in his chair and sighed. "She was a beautiful woman."

Lexi squeezed her father's knee affectionately. "Dad says sometimes when he looks at me, it's like she never left."

Michelle never knew how to ask what happened to the woman. Lexi, and certainly Jacob, never brought her up. All Michelle gathered was that when Lexi was about five, they had gone somewhere and her mother took off. Jacob acted like it did not really bother him too much, but maybe he hid the hurt he was feeling for Lexi's sake.

Lexi and Michelle turned back to the business of separating the mountain scenes from other pictures. Whenever Michelle found a likely prospect, she held it up and Lexi would shake her head. They were half-way through Lexi's stash, when Michelle suggested, "If you have the dream again, see if you can remember if the guy's got any jewelry. You know, like a ring or a watch or something you might recognize. Maybe he's wearing a shirt or a hat with a town or a sports team's name on it."

"I didn't think about anything like that. I mean, I know he's wearing boots and jeans. I think he's got a black cowboy hat on, too." Lexi frowned. It was difficult just trying to recall the bits and pieces she wrote in the journal. "I'll try to remember if there's anything that could help us." It was strange, but she was certain she would be having the dream again.

Lexi put another picture back in the box and she picked up the next one and held it up. She scooted over closer to the lamp and held it under the light. Handing it to her dad, she asked, "Where was this? The trail… I don't know. Look where Mom's standing. See that little ledge beside her?" She looked up at her father. "Dad, I think that's the place where I start running in my dream." She never remembered the beginning of the trail. It always began with her on the path and running up through the edge of the tree line.

Jacob's blood froze and he fought not to change his expression. "I don't really remember, Lexi. We took so many trips." Calming his nerves, he tried to sound disinterested, and shrugged. "Maybe Wyoming or Montana?"

"Dad, try to remember. I really think that's the place." Lexi took the picture and handed it to Michelle. "See that ledge she's standing by? That looks like the path where the guy starts chasing me. You can't see the clearing at the top, but I'm almost sure this is it. Maybe the dream *is* just a memory."

"Are the pictures in any kind of order? Like the one before or after being on the same trail?" Michelle asked.

"No, these have been shuffled through so often." Lexi's eyes narrowed on the photo. "Let's take out the pictures where Mom's wearing the same shirt," she suggested.

"Good idea. Maybe we can see something that tells us where she was that day," Michelle agreed.

Jacob stared at the television, tuning out the game. He was completely focused on the girls' find. He knew exactly where the damn picture was taken. He had not been able to get Vanessa more than a mile from that trail for the six months before she left them. *This is bad… real bad.* His hand swiped through his shaggy gray hair. It had a lot more black in it when the picture on the Pryor Mountain trail was taken.

54

There were three more photos with Vanessa wearing the same outfit and the girls struck pay dirt on the last one. Lexi and her mother were standing next to a weathered wooden sign that read, 'Wooten's Trail'. Jacob stifled a moan.

Chapter III

The girls ran to Lexi's room and booted up the computer. Even with Lexi's slow dial-up connection, they had their answer in ten minutes. Michelle tapped the zoom in button several times on the map. "Look, Lexi." She felt an unexplainable surge of excitement. "Wooten's Trail is in southwest Montana, near a boundary of the Pryor Mountain Range."

She panned out the view and they saw that Yellowstone was nearby on the northwest border of Wyoming and the Big Horn Recreation area ran through the Pryor Mountains. Most of it seemed to be color coded as BLM land, with the Crow Indian Reservation running along the eastern side of the mountains and out onto the flatlands.

"This is so cool." Michelle focused on the index at the bottom of the map. "Lexi, there's white water rafting, fishing, trail riding… that's it. Let's go there for our vacation. We can check out Wooten's Trail and it's close to Yellowstone. Jackson Hole is nearby, and that's supposed to be great."

Lexi's eyes seemed transfixed on the spot where the trail was located. "It could be nothing. Are you sure you want to spend our first grown up getaway chasing a dream?" She finally pulled her eyes away from the screen and looked at Michelle. "And, I do mean a dream," Lexi reminded her. Still, something nagged at her, just out of reach. And yet, there was a feeling of victory and trepidation.

"Absolutely," Michelle assured her. "The last real protected herd of wild mustangs is in the Pryor Mountains. People stood up to BLM about forty years ago, and they still try to block the roundups and sending them to auction." Michelle might not be able to talk her folks into taking in the mustangs, but she was just as passionate as Lexi about trying to see them in good homes.

Lexi's gaze floated from the computer screen, to a photo of Daisy-May she tacked up on the board over the desk. Her eyes always began to fill with tears when she looked at the painful reminder. Her father had taken it a week after the halter had been removed. The eyes staring out from the picture were wild with terror, but the freeze brand was clearly visible showing the cryptic markings from the BLM.

Lexi wiped her eyes and pointed to Daisy-May's neck, where the hieroglyphic marking shone white against her coat. "It's a Wyoming brand, and even though most of the Pryor Mountain mustang land is in Montana and they're supposed to be protected, I think I remember that the BLM managed to push an auction through a few years ago near Lovell. Do you think I'm having the dreams because of Daisy-May?"

Michelle studied the picture and tried to avoid staring at the raw wounds on the mustang's muzzle. "First of all, I doubt she's a Pryor Mountain Mustang. Look at the wide stance of her legs, and she doesn't have striping on her legs or withers. Besides, like you said, they hardly ever go to auction."

Lexi continued to stare at the picture, and Michelle said softly, "I know you were upset about her condition, but you've had bad cases delivered before and it never caused you to have dreams." She shook her head. "No, I think this is something else."

After a few keystrokes and waiting for a download, Michelle pointed to pictures of the mustangs grazing and frolicking on rolling foothills at the base of the mountains. "Gosh Lexi, can you imagine watching them run in the wild? Say yes, and I'll start making the plans." Michelle was printing out contact information, not waiting for an answer. Inside, something told her it was important for them to make this trip.

"It's halfway across the country. I'm not sure I can afford that much." Lexi had about fifteen hundred saved. Now, her eyes were scanning the information Michelle handed to her, and she felt a wave of anxiousness flow through her, urging her to say yes.

"Come on, Lexi," Michelle pleaded. "We can bring our own camping gear and we'll save bunches over staying at hotels. It will certainly be cheaper than Las Vegas or New York," she reasoned.

Lexi wasn't keen on those two suggestions, anyway. The thought of big concrete cities and all those people, panicked her. Besides, she didn't exactly have the kind of wardrobe for fancy places like that. "Okay, that's the plan then." She glanced towards the living room, where the sounds of the game on the television could be heard. "I'll wait until you set up the dates to tell my dad. Remember, it has to be the Monday after auction and I'll have to return the week before Dad has to bring the horses back." Lexi was not looking forward to telling her dad at all.

"No problem. How about we celebrate our birthday in Jackson Hole?" Michelle suggested. "Afterwards, we can drive through Yellowstone and hike for a few days, and then drive on to find Wooten's Trail the second week." She was already busy planning their schedule.

Michelle's birthday was July seventh and Lexi's was July eighth. They were born exactly five minutes apart, on opposite sides of midnight. Since they were seven years old they had celebrated their birthdays with a sleepover every year. Peggy, Michelle's mom, had always planned a huge blow-out at their place when they were kids. She had a birthday cake for each of them, and when Lexi was ten, she overheard Peggy tell another woman how hard it must be to be raised without a mother.

Lexi remembered wandering to the side of the barn and crying. She had not thought of her mom for a long time. Peggy found her there and hugged her until she was all cried out. She took the shiny sleeve of her silk blouse, wiped Lexi's face, and walked with her back to the party.

Even at ten years old, Michelle understood kindness to others. In return for her mother's compassion towards Lexi, Michelle gave back to her mom. Peggy had bought a birthday princess crown and Michelle wore it proudly, curtsying in her blue jeans and acting every ounce the princess... and never even once asking for whiskers. The girls would always spend the next day at Lexi's house, riding horses with their friends all day.

The birthday princess crown was slightly frayed and faded and missing some glitter. It was in a box on the top-shelf of Michelle's closet. Every year when they were younger Michelle would wear it all-day, and then hand it over to Lexi while the clock chimed twelve. As they got older, Michelle simply passed it to her to signify another year of their friendship. This year, the girls would turn twenty-one.

They discussed vacation plans until they were too tired to stay awake. Looking forward to dreams of the mountains and herds of wild Spanish mustangs, they changed into nightshirts and climbed into Lexi's double bed.

"Lexi, wake up." Michelle was softly nudging her friend while she thrashed under the covers.

Running up the dark trail, she could feel her boots scrabbling across loose pebbles. She was too close to the ledge. The sound of galloping hooves was getting louder, drowning out the footsteps of the man chasing her. The hollow moan of the wolf calling from the clearing sounded. She counted by the beat of her footfalls up the path, waiting for the howl of the wolf from the trees. There was only the sound of the clamoring horses charging up the trail.

Her foot slipped and the skittering patter of loose rocks cascaded down the side of the mountain. A hand grabbed hers just as she slid over the ledge, gripping tightly and steadily pulling her to the top. "Who are you?" Her voice echoed a fearful cry, and she felt a strip of thin leather with a knot or a bead on his wrist. "Is this Wooten's Trail? Please, I need to know." The man never answered. As soon as she claimed purchase on the ledge, he released her wrist.

She struggled to pull herself up and after scrambling onto the path, she looked along the dark trail. No one was there, and even the rhythmic uproar of the stampeding horses had silenced. The moon broke through the clouds shining a path from the top of the trail to her boots. Claws of terror scraped down her back as she studied the ground in front of her. Dug into the dirt, it said, 'YES'.

Lexi sat up so abruptly Michelle gave a startled gasp. She trembled and said, "Oh my gosh, are you okay? I couldn't get you to wake up and I almost called for your dad."

Lexi was not in any better shape, and she quivered so hard her teeth chattered. "Michelle, it *is* Wooten's Trail. I asked the man and he didn't answer, but when I got to the top, he had written 'YES' in the dirt." Lexi gripped the tail of her braid and ran her fingers through the ends. "Let me see. Oh yeah, he had a piece of leather with something tied to it on his wrist. This is so weird." Lexi shivered. "It's creeping me out a little." Actually, it was more than just a little. She found herself being drawn to the place, even though she was fully awake.

Lexi switched on the light and grabbed the photos on the desk to study them. "I'm sure it's the spot in the picture." She pointed to the ledge she had seen just a moment ago; the ledge she fell over in her dream. "Michelle, maybe this is nothing, but it's just so strange." She wrote frantically in her journal, trying to remember it all. The knowledge that she had been there when she was a child, didn't comfort her. Something about Wooten's Trail, was calling to her to come back.

The young women thumbed through the dream diary, seeing glimpses of more information unfolding. Quickly recorded was the chase up the path, the trees and wolves, and ending at the ring of fire. There was no mention at all of the horses. Lexi never remembered the thundering herd... or the Indian silhouetted against the night sky looking down on her.

Michelle smiled and gave her a hug. "Now I *know* this is vacationland. I mean, how cool is this!" She couldn't wait to decode the mystery. In the back of her mind, Michelle realized it was more than that. She really needed to find Wooten's Trail, too.

The girls talked for a while until their nerves settled, and Lexi closed her journal. Yawning, they finally lay down and managed to drift back to sleep.

The buzzing of the alarm woke them at five, and Lexi scrambled to the kitchen to make the coffee before her dad concocted another pot of sludge. After a quick breakfast, Lexi took care of Daisy-May, Travis, and Judas, her dad's horse. Jacob and Michelle loaded the last of the auction horses into the trailer and they were on their way by six thirty.

The auction parking lot was a field outside the arena, and it was filled with a good-natured gathering of familiar faces. McMillan followed behind them, towing his two-horse trailer behind a Cadillac convertible older than Lexi. He showed up without Brutus. Lexi laughed and called over, "By the time you actually do sell him, he'll be too old to walk into the ring,"

Mac slapped his straw cowboy hat on his thigh and looked sheepishly towards the ground. "Well, the mare kicked him pretty good so I don't think he'll try it again." Mac's friends knew he would never sell his favorite horse, just like they knew the mustang would be welcome to live out her days running wild through his pasture. Mac already told Lexi he would not risk training the horse and breaking her spirit. If Lexi's gentle method did not calm her, she would either come around on her own or he would enjoy watching from his porch while she taunted Brutus.

Mac had taken the mustang from the rescuers six months ago. Even with his calm patience and Lexi trying, they still could not get near her. She returned to her stall in the evenings to feed, and Mac did not push her further.

When the rescue team turned her over to Mac, it had taken a week of painful cleaning and antibiotics to get the wound to start healing. Once the danger of infection passed, Mac opened the stall door to her small fenced pasture and she never let him touch her again. The man who had originally won the bid for the pretty mare, had tried to cut the BLM freeze brand off her neck to avoid the yearlong wait to get title for her.

"I got a couple for you to ride if you have time." Mac waved his hand towards the two tethered horses. "The buckskin's gentle, but the gray's a little jumpy. I can saddle her so you can give her a try."

"Is that the gray you bought two months ago?" Lexi remembered the skittish horse and she knew what the problem was.

"Same one." Mac looked at his boots and sighed. "I was hoping to calm her down myself. I probably should have just brought her to you last month, because she's not much better now," he admitted.

"I won't have any problems with her, but let's put her up first so she doesn't get any more nervous. How about twenty-five a horse, if they sell?" The buckskin was drab with no appeal and the gray would take a selective buyer. Mac placed a minimum bid on the horses he brought to auction, because Jacob wasn't always inside the arena to place a 'rescue bid' if the offering price was too low. With Lexi riding horses she'd trained, Jacob never bothered with a minimum bid, because the horses always brought good money.

"Sounds good." Mac shook her hand and wandered off to handle the paperwork, and to find prospective horses to bid on. With Lexi riding his hoses, he figured he'd have two empty spots to fill in his trailer for the ride home.

Lexi entered the ring on the gray mare. Someone had whipped the poor animal and any quick movement by the side of her head caused her to side-step. Lexi spent five minutes getting the horse used to a short rein so nothing would catch her eye, and she kept away from the crowd riding in the center of the ring. All said and done, Mac got nine hundred for her. It was a four-hundred dollar profit over what he had paid.

Michelle leaned over the wood fence of the arena ring and watched Lexi ride. Glancing down, she rubbed the dust off the toe of her boot on the back of her jeans. Michelle could manage to ride the auction horses, but she was no trainer. Lexi had been working the green horses for years, and she could pick out weaknesses and played to their good points. Most of Michelle's quarter horses were well-trained by the time she rode them.

The few times she let Lexi talk her into riding, Michelle could feel the crowd's eyes on her and it made her nervous. She knew that her presentation looked stiff and uncomfortable, and even though she tried to relax, she never seemed to be able to sync her rhythm with the horse. They never brought high dollar and it made her feel guilty after all the time and effort Lexi put into training the horses.

Michelle's last ride was on a little dun gelding that stumbled and kept throwing its head. Mac placed a 'rescue bid' on it or a woman was getting the horse for her fifty dollar offer, and Jacob would lose more than he had earned on Lexi's last ride. Ultimately, it cost Jacob one hundred dollars to buy his own horse back. Two weeks later, Lexi rode the dun in an auction near Ocala and they tripled their money.

Michelle grew bored after watching Lexi ride a few horses through the auction, and she decided to mingle with the people outside and get away from the stifling heat and dust for a while. She walked between the horse trailers talking to several people she knew from the area. A couple of them recognized her from the Blackhawk Ranch, and they asked if she had brought any of her quarter horses with her. Although it was unlikely the superior animals would end up at the auction, there was always a chance of a good buy. Michelle informed them she was there with Lexi, and she continued her walk.

She passed Jacob a few times while he was checking out possible purchases. Once, when she got within earshot, he called her over. "So, you girls solve your mystery about that trail yet?" He hoped Michelle had not caught the slight nervous tremor in his voice.

"No, sir. We found out it's in Montana, though. It's at the edge of Pryor Mountain Range and the trail still exists." Michelle needed to get out of this conversation fast. Lexi had to be the one to tell her dad about the upcoming vacation. She searched her mind for something to say. "Um, there's a paint two trailers over that looks pretty good. He needs a little weight put on him, but he's young and an easy sixteen hands." She pointed, trying to change the subject. "He's over there."

Jacob didn't answer. He was staring over her shoulder and she turned to see what he was looking at. She caught sight of one blue-jeaned leg and cowboy boot, before it disappeared behind a pick-up truck. "Who's that?"

Jacob shook his head as if trying to clear cobwebs. "Thought it was someone I recognized. Maybe not." He put his hand on her shoulder and smiled. "Where'd you say that paint was tied?"

Michelle noticed Jacob was still glancing at where the man had been. "Over there, behind the blue trailer," she answered, and she watched Jacob walk in the direction she had pointed.

Dang. Michelle figured she better get out of the parking area, and hopefully avoid any more conversation about Lexi's trail before she blew it and mentioned the trip. Thinking of Lexi and the arena, she walked over to the concession trailer and bought two sweet teas. After the dusty rides and heat, Lexi would be ready for one.

Michelle stood in line behind a few people and turned to survey the parking area. She caught glimpses of Jacob wandering between the horse trailers. *Well, if he's going to stay out here, I'll just have to stay inside the arena.* Jacob was taking his time, talking to people and studying their horses. By the looks of things, it would be awhile before she would be able to escape to the fresh air again.

Chapter IV

Michelle paid for the drinks and walked into the arena. Lexi was cantering the little black gelding she liked in an easy lope around the barrels. She finished her ride and walked the horse towards the exit gate, and Michelle changed course towards where she was dismounting.

A man's a deep voice called out from behind her. "Is your friend the one that hires out for riding?"

Michelle turned around. "Yes, that's Lexi." She stopped in her tracks about three feet away from one all-out drop-dead gorgeous cowboy. The guy had seriously deep green eyes, the perfect 'forgot to shave this morning beard', and shaggy blonde hair curling around his ears under his cowboy hat, to say nothing of that killer body in those tight jeans… and Michelle had absolutely no idea why she hated the auctions anymore. "Um, I can introduce you if you'd like. I was just bringing her a drink."

"That'd be great. I'm here by myself and it'd be too confusing trying to handle the bidding and riding," he said with a smile.

Oh, and yes, beautiful bright white teeth with the perfect full lips... snap out of it girl. "I'm Michelle."

"Brent." He tipped his hat. "Good to meet you." They made their way over to where Lexi stood with the black horse.

A girl with red braids and a bright blue cowboy hat stroked her hand down the gelding's neck, adoration filling her hazel eyes. "Is this your first horse?" Lexi smiled, knowing the girl would be a perfect match.

The girl nodded without taking her eyes off the horse. "But, I've practiced running barrels on my grandpa's pony and I get to help when we take in a mustang."

Lexi looked over to a smiling older man and she recognized him from the rescue team. Sam Morrison was a widower, and his granddaughter had been left on his doorstep a few years ago. Lexi patted the gelding's neck. "Well, he certainly likes you."

The girl looked up at her, beaming. "I think so, too." Her sparkling eyes became serious. "You just wait, Miss Lexi. I'll be riding good as you, next year."

Lexi laughed. "I bet you will, Cindy. He's going to make a fine barrel horse." Handing over the reins, Lexi watched the girl lead the gelding away. She was pleased he was going to such a nice home.

Sam called over, "I'll get the saddle and tack back to you."

"Don't worry about it, Mr. Morrison. I'll get it from you at the next auction." Lexi smiled and watched Cindy, already mounted and riding towards the parking area. She figured Sam would be lucky to get her off the horse and into his truck for the ride home.

Turning to Michelle, she took the iced tea and gulped a few swallows. "Gosh, thanks. I have half the dirt of the ring in my mouth, right now." She looked over at the horse and his enamored new owner. Her gray-blue eyes narrowed with satisfaction. "But damn if he didn't shine on the barrels. Dad paid five hundred for him last month and we just sold him for twelve." Lexi would get an additional hundred fifty from her dad for that ride.

"Lexi, this is Brent. He wanted to talk to you about riding for him." Michelle stood next to the cowboy, staking her claim on the unsuspecting man.

Lexi held out her hand. "Good to meet you. Depending on the horse, I charge twenty-five or thirty-five. How broke are they?"

"If you have time, I'd like you to look at them. They're not really mine. I drove down to settle my uncle's estate and these were the last of the horses. The rest I managed to sell to private owners, but the auction will be quicker for these," Brent explained.

Lexi turned to check the number on the current horse being offered. "Sure, I have a little break now." Lexi followed Brent and Michelle over to a horse trailer with a for sale sign on it. The cowboy reached up and pulled it off.

"I sold it and forgot to take this off. I got lucky with that. I really just want to finish this stuff and get home. The ranch is with a realtor and these five horses are the end of it." Brent backed one of the horses out.

Lexi ran her hands over the horse's body, checking for weaknesses. The horse appeared to be well mannered and completely calm while she examined it for any potential problems. "Are they all like this? This guy's very well trained." She lifted the horse's leg to check its hoof.

"Pretty much. I think my uncle only used them for pleasure horses. You know, for company and stuff," Brent answered.

"Twenty-five a horse and you handle the paperwork. Piece of cake." Lexi smiled. The horses would practically sell themselves and she'd earn an extra one hundred twenty five dollars.

"You said you were anxious to get home. Where's that?" Michelle was a little depressed that the cowboy wasn't a local.

"It's a long way from here." His green eyes turned to the west. "I have a place in Montana." Brent walked into the trailer to unload the rest of the horses and tie them off.

Lexi and Michelle stared at each other. Michelle followed him inside and took the lead rope to one of the horses. "Montana?" she repeated.

"Yeah, my friend has a ranch up there and we raise cattle," he replied.

"What part of Montana?" Michelle pressed. "I mean which side of the state?"

He smiled down at her and she melted. "Why? Have you been there? The ranch is on the southern border near the Big Horn Recreation area."

"Okay, this is really weird. Lexi and I are planning a vacation next month out there. Actually, we're planning on going into Jackson Hole to celebrate our birthdays. After that we're hiking through Yellowstone, and then driving over to the Pryor Mountains. There's a place called Wooten's Trail we're going to check out." *Maybe I will get to see this luscious guy again, after all*, Michelle thought.

"It's pretty up there." The man placed his hand on her shoulder, completely focusing on her, and seeming to search for something in her eyes. "You gotta' be careful though. It's not maintained as well as some of the more popular places." His hand dropped back to his side.

"You've been there? You've been to the trail?" Michelle resisted the urge to put his hand back on her shoulder. Something felt very right about the cowboy, and she could almost imagine having the gooey feelings her friends described about their boyfriends.

Brent shrugged, breaking the spell, and he untied the last horse for Lexi to look at. She seemed immersed in accessing the horses, and Brent turned back to Michelle. "Sure, the beginning's a few miles from the ranch. I like to go riding up there sometimes. The mountains are a refuge for wild horses, and I like watching them. When were you two planning on coming out?"

"We want to leave for Wyoming in time for our birthdays, so we should be in Montana the middle of July. We're still figuring out travel and lodging. We can camp on the trail, but we need a starting point to leave some gear and the car," Michelle replied.

Actually, Lexi was listening attentively while checking out the horses. She knew when Michelle was on a mission, and just like setting up the potential adoptions for the mustangs, Michelle was much better at dealing with people. Although, it seemed this guy had her practically stuttering, and Lexi thought it was amusing. He was a handsome cowboy, but nothing that made her all gaga like her friend.

"Look, why don't I give you my number? You can give me a heads up call when you're coming and Nicholas and I can guide you up there. You can leave your extra gear at the ranch," Brent offered. "Trust me, you'll appreciate being on horseback instead of trying to hike the whole thing."

"That sounds great." Michelle thought her little plan worked out better than she'd hoped. She had a weird feeling of excitement about seeing him again, and an even stranger feeling of a loss so great that her stomach cramped, at the thought of him leaving. *Gosh, if this is what a crush feels like, no thank you. I'm almost twenty-one and behaving like a high school kid.*

Lexi frowned at Michelle's odd behavior. "Yes, thank you for the offer, Brent. I was actually up there once before when I was a kid, but I don't remember it."

"It's settled then." Brent walked to his truck and came back with a business card. Lexi gave Michelle a sideways glance as she practically drooled when the cowboy smiled at her. "That's the ranch house number and this one's my cell. I'll let Nicholas know in case you call and I'm out."

Lexi was leading the last of Brent's horses into the ring, and he excused himself from Michelle's side. He told her he would be right back, and he explained that he had left something in his truck. As soon as Brent walked out to the parking area, he flipped open his phone. It was answered on the second ring, and Brent imagined that Nicholas had been anxiously pacing the floor, waiting for his call. "Hi, how are things back home?"

"Good, how are things on your end?" Nicholas walked out onto the porch and looked towards the mountains. He imagined Vanessa sitting near the caves with Aaron, and his eyes narrowed with a satisfied smile. Silas had easily pried the location of her daughter from her, and his kid brother would suffer with the knowledge their mate would soon be back in the mountains, yet forever out of his reach.

Some thought Nicholas and Aaron were identical, but Nicholas always considered his younger twin possessed all of their weaknesses, while he held all their strength. And, Nicholas despised weakness. To have it so flagrantly staring back at him through his own likeness was annoying. Nicholas continued to look towards the cliffs while he refocused on Brent's words. "What?"

"I said, better than we planned," Brent replied. "It seems she figured out Wooten's Trail and already planned a trip in July. We could have saved the money on these horses I picked up in Mississippi." He laughed as he considered the time they had spent arranging the props for this meeting. There was silence from the other end, and Brent stifled his amusement. Apparently, Nicholas did not share his humor.

"Damn." Mentally, Nicholas tallied up the tab for the excursion. "How much did you get for the horses?"

Shit. Brent knew Nicholas could be a real pain most of the time. "We're a hundred over cost, and there's still the last one being bid on, now."

"Well, you're getting paid for transporting the trailer and truck to that guy in Jacksonville, so we should break about even." Nicholas thought about the wasted time figuring out where to get the horses to bring to auction, just so Brent could meet Lexi. They had struggled for weeks to fabricate a believable story, and now it seemed none of it had been necessary. Naturally, he blamed Brent for suggesting the ruse. And of course, none of it would have been necessary, if Jacob had not run off with the girl. Nicholas glared towards the mountain, picturing Vanessa again. He hoped her leg was throbbing.

"She's bringing a friend, a little cutie named Michelle. She's going to call us when they're coming out, and I told them we'd guide them up the trail."

Nicholas' continued to stare at the mountain. He couldn't wait to present Lexi to her mother and Aaron as his mate. "Oh, we'll do that alright," he chuckled. "I'll see you in about a week, then?"

"Yes." Brent peeled his shirt away from his chest. "You wouldn't believe how hot it is down here. I can't wait to get out of this swamp and back to the mountains." He looked in the direction of the arena and frowned. "Hey Nicholas, is there a chance we have one missing?" Brent had been feeling slightly uneasy since he first laid eyes on Michelle.

"What do you mean? You think you found another female?"

"Yeah, I got a funny feeling when I met that friend of hers."

"I haven't heard anything, but I'll check and get back to you," Nicholas offered. He had no intention of inquiring. Brent was not sent on a mission to pick up strays.

"Do that, okay? Make sure to check with Paul, and I'll see you soon." They said their goodbyes and Brent walked back to the ring to pay Lexi. His eyes immediately sought a golden ponytail, and Michelle turned and smiled at him. *God, no. It can't be.* The frozen lump in his gut told him different.

The last of the auction horses sold, and Michelle stood gazing into Brent's green eyes. "Well, it was good to meet you. I'll give you a call sometime next month, when Lexi and I have the trip planned. Is there any time that won't be good for you and your friend?"

"No, summer pretty well takes care of itself unless there's a drought. Anytime should work." Brent watched Lexi put the tack into the trailer. "You said you were going to Jackson Hole and Yellowstone first?"

Michelle nodded and followed his gaze. "Lexi and I celebrate our birthdays together, and we figure we could party in Jackson Hole before we headed out." Michelle noticed with dismay the attentive way Brent watched her friend. She felt sick and angry with herself for being jealous.

Brent turned back to Michelle, tilting his head as if studying her curiously. He smiled, and she relaxed. "Then, you're planning to stay for about a week in Montana?"

Jacob was loading the six horses he had purchased, and he finally got the last stubborn horse tied in when he overheard the end of their conversation. "A week for what?" he asked. Jacob looked at Michelle, and then his eyes passed over her to the cowboy.

Michelle was dumbfounded and desperately tried to get Lexi's attention so she could come bail her out. She stared at her as she swung another saddle into the trailer, and willed her to turn and look at her. With her attention focused on Lexi, Michelle missed the uneasy expression on Jacob's face when he walked up to the man and held out a hand. "Jacob Weston, and you are?"

"Brent Stromwell. It's good to meet you." Brent stared Jacob straight in the eyes and noticed he winced uneasily at the name.

Michelle finally ran up to the front of the trailer to get Lexi. "We got trouble, girl. Your dad overheard Brent and me talking about this summer."

"Shoot, I better get over there." Lexi and Michelle walked quickly back to the two men. They stopped about five feet away, noticing a sort of standoff between them. "What the heck?" Lexi had never seen her father take such an aggressive stance with a stranger before.

"Montana?" Jacob asked suspiciously. "What brings you down here?"

"I had an estate matter to settle, and a little research project for a friend." Brent smiled and nodded towards the girls. "Turns out it was a lucky chance meeting, as your two girls are heading out our way this summer."

Jacob looked at the man… and he *knew*. He straightened and clenched his jaws and fists. "The hell they are, mister."

Brent lowered his voice. "Jacob, you know you can't stop this. She's getting the dreams, isn't she? How else would she know about the trail?" His green eyes briefly flashed amber.

This is it, then, Jacob thought. He turned and saw the confused look on the girls' faces. "Lexi, Michelle, in the truck," he ordered. When the girls silently walked away, Jacob turned back to Brent. "She's only twenty one. I got four more years." His hands curled and loosened in frustration. The instinct to fight and protect was strong, but the real enemy was the mountain. "They got my Vanessa. They ain't getting' my daughter."

Brent put his hands up in mock surrender. "Hey, don't shoot the messenger." He was uncomfortable with the weary determination in the older man's eyes. The fact that it was Nicholas waiting… well, he wouldn't think about that right now. "You can't stop this, Jacob. No one can. That girl will end up walking to Montana, if you try to keep her here."

Brent wasn't surprised at Jacob's anger. He just knew how useless his words were. "Vanessa told you what would happen, Jacob. Her father was an elder and you should be leader right now. You knew you shouldn't have taken Lexi out of the mountains." Brent could see the desperation in the man's face. He said softly, "Hell, Jacob, come with her. Come back to the Baáhpuuo and spend your time with Vanessa, watching the iichíile running free. You never should have left."

Jacob was uncomfortable this stranger knew so much about him. He thought he had covered his tracks over the years, always keeping a low profile. "This business doesn't have anything to do with Lexi." He fought tears, and added, "Tell Vanessa she can't have her."

"It isn't Vanessa that's pulling her. You know that. Jacob, you try to stop those girls from coming out and you'll lose your daughter, just like you lost your wife.

You might do better explaining to Lexi what's going on. If you don't, this summer's going to be a lot harder on her." Brent turned, and he gave a slight tip to his cowboy hat. Before he walked off, he looked back. "Jacob, it's not me. I wish it were, but it's not." He turned and walked back towards his truck.

Jacob stared after him for a few seconds, and then slowly made his way back to the pickup. He needed time to think this out, and he was not looking forward to the ride home.

The girls had been fidgeting in the cab, waiting for Jacob. "Michelle, Brent's going to tell Dad all about our plans. I wanted to break it to him slowly. We're probably going to end up arguing the whole way back to the ranch now." Lexi nervously watched through the side mirror while the two men talked. She saw her dad coming back to the truck while Brent walked away.

The door opened and Jacob climbed in. He was silent for a moment, gazing at nothing through the windshield. Gripping the key, he plunged it into the ignition, pumping the gas pedal a few times until the diesel chugged to life. "I don't want to talk about this right now. We'll discuss it when we get home."

"Dad, I'm sorry. Michelle and I just started talking about this last night, after we found the picture." Lexi twisted her hands together nervously.

"Lexi, please, when we get home." He turned onto the small rural highway leading back to the ranch.

The ride was silent, as everybody's minds filled with explanations. Michelle looked out the window, Lexi looked down at her lap trying to figure out how to convince her dad to let them go on the trip, and Jacob stared straight ahead, lips tight in concentration. Lexi thought he was angry. Actually, Jacob was trying to figure out a way to stop the inevitable. He truly believed getting Lexi far away from the mountain would save her. How wrong he was.

They dropped Michelle off at her house, and she mouthed, 'I'll call you tomorrow,' to Lexi. It was just passed dark when they pulled into Sunchaser, and Jacob jumped out and began unloading the horses. Lexi walked over to help him, and he said, "Lexi, just go on in the house. I need to think about this. We'll talk in the morning."

"I'm sorry, Dad. Please don't be mad at me."

He could hear the pain in her voice at the thought she had hurt him, and he turned to see tears threatening to spill. Jacob could not stand that. This was not her fault. "I'm not mad at you, honey. It's just tough watching you grow up." He tried to smile. "My stubborn old head has to sort it out." Jacob hugged her, and then looked into her eyes. "You, go on in and get some sleep. It's been a long day."

"Okay, Daddy." Lexi kissed his cheek and strolled slowly towards the house, kicking blades of grass.

"Lexi?"

"Yes, Dad?" She turned to see her father smiling at her, and she knew everything would be alright.

"That was a good call on the barrels for that black gelding. It was a nice ride." He knew she had put a lot of extra time on the horse.

"Thanks, Dad." Lexi smiled and picked up her pace as she walked to her room.

Jacob led the last auction horse into the pasture and wandered into the barn. He walked passed Travis and Judas to the stall on the end. Slowly holding out his hand, the horse stepped forward and rubbed its nose against his palm. "How you doing tonight, Daisy-May?"

He scooped some feed for her, filled her water, and added another flat of hay to the net. The entire time, the horse stood still, staring at him. Jacob looked at the halter, a deeper blue in the shadows, but a definite first place prize for the small mustang. "She's done well by you. It's a shame our brothers could not get the restrictions in the Red Desert out there in Wyoming that we got on the Pryor range. But you'll have a good life now, just as we promised."

Jacob left the barn and gazed across the quiet pastures at the new horses, grazing and milling around while they learned their new surroundings. He inhaled the heavy humid Florida night and sighed. Weariness seemed to crush him while he considered the fifteen year sacrifice he and Vanessa had made to protect Lexi. They should have known it would do no good.

The lights in her room were off, but Jacob thought he could hear her moaning through the opened window. "The damn dreams," he muttered. He knew they would only get worse, and he was powerless to stop them.

* * * *

The man chased her up the mountain, and she did not try to talk to him this time. The horses galloped faster and she tried not to panic. She was determined to go further into the dream. Just before she got to the clearing, she looked up and down the trail.

Her legs seemed to move on their own volition towards the fire, and she walked to within ten feet and saw someone else standing by the circle of flames. It was an older version of herself, with a large grey wolf sitting beside her. "Come to me, honey," the woman called. "Lexi, come back to me."

Lexi looked at the woman, but she did not move towards her. Something about moving ahead made her very nervous. The wolf was gone and the man with the dark hair was standing silently beside her. Lexi glanced back down the trail, and she saw her father standing about fifty feet away with silent tears washing down his tanned cheeks. A herd of horses stood behind him, with the stallion pawing the ground. Her father called out, "Come back. Lexi, please come back to me."

Jacob was standing over her bed, shaking her shoulders and trying to break the trance she was in. "Lexi, please come back to me. Come on, honey, wake up." When he had woken to her moaning and walked into her room, his face turned ashen at the familiar expression on her face. It was the same expression he had seen so many times on Vanessa, when he tried to take her from the mountains and the night spirits wrestled in her mind.

"Dad?" Lexi struggled awake. At some point she had begun crying in her sleep. "Daddy, what's going on? I think I saw Mom in my dream. She had a wolf sitting next to her, and she wanted me to come to her. It scared me." The chalk pallor to her face and trembling voice attested to her fear.

Jacob sat down on the bed and held her. "Oh, baby, I'm so sorry. It's alright. It's going to be alright." He switched on the light. "Come on out to the living room. I think we need to talk."

Chapter V

Lexi was still shaking when she followed him out to the other room. "Wait here," Jacob said, and he walked down the hallway towards his bedroom.

Lexi sat down on the sofa, folding her legs beneath her and wrapping the quilt around her shoulders. Even in the heat, she felt chilled. She tried to calm her nerves, and she wondered what her father wanted to tell her.

Jacob walked into his room, opened the closet door, and let his fingers trail over the loose panel on the back wall of his closet that camouflaged his hidey-hole. There was no more putting this off, and he knew it. As his fingers worked the panel loose, he thought of how many years he had wasted being apart from Vanessa.

On top of the leather-bound book, laid the stack of photos he had hidden yesterday. He picked them up and stared into his wife's eyes. Vanessa was smiling and standing behind her little girl, with her arms draped over Lexi's shoulders. It was the last day they were together, and Jacob could almost hear Vanessa's soft voice whisper, *Not wasted, Jacob. Not if it had worked.* His finger brushed down her cheek, and he whispered, "But, it didn't, Vanessa. It didn't work. Lexi's having the dreams."

Jacob lifted the old book and placed the pictures inside the back cover. If Lexi had been raised on the mountain, he would not have this hollow feeling in his stomach. He would not have to risk Lexi hating him, when he finally told her the truth. She would probably blame him, but he hoped she would understand that he and her mom had done what they thought they could to protect her.

Lexi looked up when her father returned a few minutes later, carrying an old leather-bound book which he placed on his chair. He sighed and walked out to the kitchen, and Lexi heard cupboard doors open. A moment later, he returned with two glasses of brandy. "Here, honey. Drink this. It'll calm you down."

It was the first time he had ever given her alcohol other than sparkling wine on New Year's Eve, after she turned eighteen. Lexi knew that whatever he was going to tell her, whatever was in that book, must be serious. She stuck the tip of her tongue into the amber liquid and felt the warm burn.

Jacob wrestled with how to begin. "Lexi, you know how I told you your mother really loved our time in the mountains," he began.

"Yes, Dad. You told me that they had some kind of power over her. Some power she could not control. You said she was miserable when you tried to get her to leave and start a life down here with us." Lexi never really understood, but she accepted her mother's decision because her father did.

"It was a little more than that, Lexi. Your mom would have killed herself if I forced her off the mountain." Jacob opened the book.

"Was she crazy, Dad? I don't know what you mean." Now she was really getting nervous, and she took a sip of the brandy. It burned her throat, all the way to her stomach.

"No honey, she wasn't crazy." He shuffled uneasily in his chair. "Lexi, I need to tell you some things; things that aren't going to make a whole lot of sense to you. Things you might not even believe. I never told you before, because I'd hoped if I got you away, you'd be safe. The pull is too strong. Even when you started having the dreams, I was hoping it would go away. But, when that cowboy, Brent, told me you two were planning on going out there… well, it's just time to tell you." Jacob studied the cover of the old book.

"You knew? When I started having the nightmares, you knew what caused them?" Lexi was confused and she studied him with wide gray eyes, picking nervously at the quilt.

Her dad looked miserable, and he nodded. "You're mom got them too, whenever we came down off that damn mountain." His hand threaded through his hair, and Lexi knew whatever he was going to tell her, he was not looking forward to it. "That's what I meant when I told you she'd have killed herself. Every night she'd get them until I took her back up there. It's why we camped so much back then. She didn't want to spend an extra minute away from you, until we had to leave."

Jacob held one of her hands. He looked like he was going to cry, and Lexi ached with the pain she saw in his eyes. "She loves you so much, Lexi. It about made her want to die, knowing she couldn't come with us, and knowing she had to send you away to try to keep you safe. She said she didn't want you stuck with the legacy. That's why she told me to take you and go, and she made me promise to take you far away from there." Her father looked so weary, and for the first time, Lexi noticed he was getting old. "Fifteen years, Lexi, and it didn't work."

"Dad, I don't understand what your trying to tell me." Tears were filling her eyes. It was the most her father had spoken about her mom in years, and he made it sound like she still loved her.

"Oh, shit," Jacob muttered, trying to compose his resolve. He glanced at the book. "Look, hear me out. I'll answer your questions, Lexi, but I'm also going to ask you not to go out there. Please, honey. Stay away from the mountain."

Lexi settled back on the couch as her dad began the story. In a wistful voice, he said, "Your mom and I were both born near those mountains. All the ranches around it have been handed down to families for generations, and I recognized Brent's last name. I knew his folks." He smiled at her surprised expression, but she didn't speak.

"No one remembers how or when we got together. We can trace most of the families back a couple hundred years, with a few new one's moving in over that time. Our community has its own little government and rules. We have to. My father was an elder, before he was shot." Jacob looked over at Lexi.

Her father had always changed the subject whenever she asked about their family. Now, her mind wandered to possible answers to what he was suggesting. *Were they some kind of religious cult?* "You told me grandpa was in a hunting accident," Lexi confirmed, trying to wade through his speech.

"Yes, Lexi. Some men shot him while he was hunting." Jacob took a sip of brandy, containing the quick burst of rage that raced through him. The bullet had instantly killed his father, and the magic the Crow held could not save him.

Lexi frowned, dragging at parts of the old story for what she could remember. It had been a long time ago, when he told her. She was young, and most of what he said made no sense to her. "You said they weren't ever prosecuted. I remember asking you about that."

"No, Lexi, they were never prosecuted." Jacob's voice was low... almost a whisper. "Our community knew who did it, and we took care of it." Jacob looked at her for a reaction.

Lexi slowly shook her head in confusion. The story was getting even more confusing. "What do you mean, Dad? Like vigilante stuff?" Lexi was trying to grasp what he was telling he, but his words seemed like a jumbled patchwork of frightening implications.

Jacob shook his head. "No, our community just has a different set of rules. See, the police never would have gone after these guys, because there wasn't a body."

"Then, how do you know he was killed? Dad, this isn't making sense." Lexi looked at the book he was absently rubbing with his thumb.

"Why do you collect wolves? You're obsessed with them. Why is that, Lexi?" Jacob watched her closely. He wasn't sure how much she gathered from the dreams.

The question caught Lexi off guard. "What? I don't know. I guess they always fascinated me. They seem so wild and confident, and I feel sorry for the way they're treated like predators and hunted. To me, they're beautiful."

Jacob pressed further. "You've had two boyfriends that I know of, and you ran both of them off. They were good guys. Why'd you do that?"

Lexi smiled. "I would think you'd be happy about that." She shrugged her shoulders under the quilt, and said, "I guess I'm just still in my 'horse' stage. I don't know, Dad. They just seemed so, so, I don't know, soft or mushy or something." She scrunched up her face. "There just wasn't any kind of an emotional thing between us. Mostly, I went out because the other girls did and I felt odd girl out on dates." Lexi realized she never really got boy crazy like some of her friends had. "Michelle doesn't date much either, you know," she countered, defensively.

Jacob knew the answer to that one, as well. Her parents, her *adoptive* parents, Peggy and Drew, spoke with him about it. Their attempts at getting Michelle interested in life around campus had failed. Peggy would have loved for her daughter to announce she was staying in Gainesville for a campus party. The couple met with Jacob and briefly questioned whether the girls were forming a more personal relationship.

Jacob had checked Michelle's background. He was unsure if Brent realized who she was yet, because he would have been expecting the scent to come from Lexi… and Michelle was only half-breed. That probably explained why she did not suffer the dreams, but Jacob wasn't really sure how her kind was affected. *Hell, maybe they don't even have the dreams.* Still, Michelle would have been influenced into pushing for the mountain trip, even if subconsciously.

The chair creaked as Jacob sat back and sighed. His fingers tapped the top of the book, and he said, "Well, I've skirted around this and through it, so I guess I'll just come out with it. Lexi, you got your mom and me in you, and getting you away from the mountains didn't do a damn bit of good. Vanessa wasn't strong enough to leave, but she was afraid you'd get hurt like your grandpa… like so many of us… if you stayed up there."

Lexi sat forward at the mention of her mom again. "Please, Dad, tell me what you mean. I don't understand what you're telling me, but I'm listening and I'll wait until you're finished."

"Some say it's a curse, others a blessing." He shrugged. "We don't know if we've always been here, like another breed of animal, or if something was changed in us later." Jacob gripped the edges of the book, bracing himself for her reaction. "We're shape-shifters, Lexi." Jacob looked down, guiltily staring at the amber liquor in his glass.

Lexi's reaction was not what he expected. She stared at him for a moment, and then burst out laughing. His head jerked up, and she said, "Jeeze, Dad. You really had me going. If you were trying to make me forget my dream, it worked."

Jacob looked at her, bewildered. He just confessed a secret he had protected her from her whole life, and she was *laughing* at him? His expression made her laugh harder, and that made him angry. "Lexi, this is no joke." She laughed harder, holding her stomach.

Jacob stood up and put the book on the table. He walked over and put an arm on either side of her and stared into her laughing face. The hair on the back of his neck bristled, and he carefully controlled his change. The last thing he wanted to do was scare her, but he knew no other way to make her understand… to make her believe.

Lexi looked into his eyes, and they changed from deep gray with the indigo striations, to an almost iridescent blue. His canines began to lengthen and his shaggy silver hair began filling over his cheeks. Lexi recoiled into the sofa cushions, and screamed.

Jacob released his grip on the back of the sofa, instantly retracting the claws that had punctured through the fabric. He walked to the kitchen and when he returned to pour her a little more brandy, his face had returned to normal. Lexi stared up at him, shaking in shocked silence as he held the glass for her to take a sip. "Come on, Lexi. That's right." He wrapped her trembling fingers around the glass, and calmly took his seat across from her.

"Now, can we continue?" He figured she probably couldn't reply, just yet. "As I said, we're shape-shifters. Our community protects the wolves and the cougars. My father was hunting in his wolf-form when he was shot, and our pack found the hunters responsible. The land they were on is protected, and they were not supposed to be there. We knew taking care of it ourselves was the only justice we would be able to get."

Lexi stared at her lap, shaking her head in denial. "I'm still dreaming, aren't I? This isn't real."

"You're not dreaming." Jacob felt a surge of angry frustration at the thought of his beautiful daughter blindly running to the mountain, and suffering the same fate as his father. "Damn it, Lexi. Listen to me. If you go back to those mountains, you're going to get caught up in this. Down here, you have a chance." His eyes fixed on her, imploring her to understand. "Here, I can help you. You don't need to hide like the rest of them," Jacob insisted.

She was staring at him, quietly lost in confusion and more than a little fear. Jacob could see residual shock beginning to wash away from her expression. Still, he figured he'd made a disaster of everything. "Look, it's late." He sighed, threaded his fingers through his hair, and said, "I think the book will explain things better than I have. I seemed to have made a total mess of things. Read through it. Ask me what you need to, but read it, Lexi. It's your history." Jacob got up and with book in hand, guided Lexi back to her room. "Do not discuss this with anybody. No one, not even Michelle." *Especially Michelle*, he thought.

Lexi sat in bed with the book in her lap, afraid to open it. She had seen her dad's face change. She knew she had, but her mind would not let her believe it. Her fingers traced over the scuffed leather surface of the book's cover until they curled under the edge and finally opened it to the pages. She read for hours, and instead of the words blurring to a crazy fantasy, she felt something deep inside filling her with a feeling of completeness. It felt like an empty cavern inside her soul was finally whole and saturated with the colors and scents of her ancestry. Lexi fell asleep with the book open on her lap, to a page with a drawing of a girl standing on a trail. A wolf was sitting beside her.

* * * *

She ran up the path with the man chasing her. When she reached the clearing, the woman was sitting by the fire with her back to her. The woman sensed Lexi's heavy breathing, and she stood up. The man had walked up behind her, by then.

The woman turned around, and a smile lit her eyes. "Lexi, I knew you'd come back."

"Mom?" Lexi's eyes filled with tears. "I don't understand. I'm so confused." The man put a comforting arm around her shoulder and molded his body up against her. Lexi leaned back into him. He felt safe.

"You will, baby. I'll see you soon, and you'll know everything. I'm here, Lexi. I'll wait for you." Her mom walked closer, and she ran a finger through the tears on Lexi's cheek. Then, she turned back towards the fire and started running. By the time she reached the other side of the flames, a wolf emerged and disappeared into one of the caves.

The man turned Lexi around and held her head against his chest until her tears stopped. She looked up and could only see the shine from the fire-flame in his eyes. The rest of his face was in shadows, hidden by the brim of his black cowboy hat. "I'm so confused. Please tell me what's happening to me," Lexi cried.

The man patiently combed his fingers through her hair, holding her gently. "It's all going to be alright."

The stallion raced by them, drew up onto his hind legs, and pawed the air with his front hooves. He stared at Lexi with wild eyes, whinnying to the other horses filling the clearing.

Chapter VI

By the time Lexi awoke, it was late morning. For once, she remembered almost everything in her dream and the feeling of fear she usually experienced, was missing. Instead, she felt edgy anticipation that the things she had seen might be real. While she dressed, she glanced over to the old book and a wave of something close to desire seemed to fill her. She wanted to be there. She wanted to be a part of it.

She ambled towards the kitchen, yawning. Because she'd slept in so late, Lexi knew her dad had already taken care of the morning chores. She found him sitting in the living room when she entered with a cup of coffee for him from the pot she had re-brewed, and she handed him a fresh cup. Before she sat down, she retrieved the book from her room and she returned to the table beside his chair.

Dropping down onto the sofa across from him, Lexi quietly sipped her coffee and snuck furtive glances at her father. In the light of day, she was not sure she believed it, but something strange was going on. There was a surge of uneasy excitement, filling her thoughts like empty pockets of memories she had been unaware of, and they began to consume her with possibilities. One thing was certain. After reading through the book and comparing some of the stories to the dreams she had been having, she knew she believed her dad... and her need to go to the mountain seemed much more desperate than the whim of a mere vacation.

Jacob watched her, silently waiting for her reaction to all that was in the book. She didn't look too upset with him, and he was relieved. What he thought he was seeing was a bit more excitement, instead of the dread he had seen on her face over the past few weeks. In her eyes, Jacob could see she wasn't afraid... and she didn't hate him. That was the thing that had worried him the most. "You okay, Lexi?"

She nodded. As close as she was to her father, she had no idea how to discuss this with him. "So, what happens now?" she asked.

"What do you mean?" Jacob rested his hand on top of the closed book. "I sure as hell wish you wouldn't take that trip this summer." Jacob watched her, and he could already see the wild heat building behind her eyes. It was the lure of the mountain he had watched come over Vanessa, and what she had read from the book was partially responsible. It was probably still better than making her go through the restless nights, consumed with dreams she didn't understand. Somehow, that didn't seem fair to her.

"I've got to go. Dad, I've dreamed things in that book. The pictures… I've seen those places and the things that are happening. Not all of them, but a few." She studied the worn leather cover. "I've never seen that book before, have I." It was more a statement than a question. Lexi was certain she would have remembered the book.

"No, honey, I figured it was best to keep it hidden until it looked like you might need to read through it, so I've kept it away from you." He could see the uncertainty in her eyes, but her sideways glances and the way she wouldn't quite look at him head-on, gave her away. "Look, I can see you're going to do this." He rifled his fingers through his hair and let out a weary, exasperated breath. "Hell, maybe you need to." Jacob sat back, defeated.

Lexi knew he could never understand what she felt from the dreams. He didn't know how they ripped apart her soul, frightening her worse than anything she had ever known, and then put her back together again with a feeling of safety and completeness. That's what was missing here. She loved her father, the horses, and Sunchaser Ranch. But, there was always a shadowing nagging that this was just a stepping-stone, while she waited to discover her true purpose. "Dad, I need to figure this out. If the dream isn't true, I can come back here and get on with my life. If it is, maybe I'll get to see Mom... maybe the mountain won't affect me the way it does her."

Oh Lexi, not with your bloodline. The only chance was to get you away and hope maybe with the distance, it couldn't get hold of you. As much as he hated to do it, Jacob knew that he had to tell her the rest of it. "If you're going, there are other things you need to know." His shoulders straightened. "Also, I'll be going with you." The thrill of thoughts of the mountain washed through him, and he tried to squash the feelings. It had been easier for him to control his need to go home, the longer he had been gone.

"Dad, it's our birthday and Michelle and I are planning to celebrate in Jackson Hole before we find the trail." Lexi was trying to think of a nice way to un-invite him.

"I won't mess with that. I know the two of you want to have some time on your own, so I'll go on up to Montana and wait for you. We'll take the month off," he decided. "Travis is ready to be delivered to Sandy, and I'll bring Judas to Mac's. Brutus could use the distraction from the mustang, anyway. We'll skip the auction in July, and you should have Daisy-May ready for placement with Amy by then."

It was obvious she was not going to deter him, and that he had already figured out a plan if he couldn't stop her. Lexi decided to give it one more try. "Are you sure? I figured if we left on a Monday, I'd be back in time to at least begin to start a few."

Jacob smiled at her hopeful expression. There was too great a chance she would not be able to leave, though. Even if the other little problem did not pan out, there was a good possibility that once Lexi returned to the mountain, she would not be able to let go of the dreams if she tried to leave… like Vanessa. "No, we'll just take the month off. Things might take longer to straighten out than your thinking they will."

Lexi resigned herself to the idea her dad was not going to be swayed from trying to protect her. Heck, she was all he had for the past fifteen years. "You said there were other things I needed to know." Lexi was curious, and she asked the uppermost concern on her mind. "Am I going to change like you do?"

"Probably, if you want to. It usually hits in your early twenties and no later than twenty-five, if you can. Some of the bloodlines got diluted with shifters mixing with non-shifters as they left the mountains to help with the mustangs, and you can't always tell with them." Jacob straightened, smiled, and he tipped his coffee cup at her. "You're pureblood though, and from the original line. They're the ones that find it toughest to stay away from the mountain for long."

He actually sounds proud, Lexi thought. "I'm pureblood what? You said wolves and cougars." She was pretty sure she knew the answer to that one, after seeing the brief flash of him beginning to change the night before

"Oh, we're wolves." This time, he *did* sound proud. "Vanessa and I, both." He closed his eyes and smiled. "You used to love to play with us when you were young; climbing all over us." He opened his eyes again and chuckled. "You had quite a grip for such a little thing. We had to stop changing around you when you turned four, and began to wonder why the dogs were never around when your mom and I were."

Jacob chuckled again, relaxing a little. "It's best not to change around the kids when they get older. They don't understand that not everybody's Mommy and

Daddy can do it." Sadness drew his features down and his ruddy jowls sagged a bit. "You'd just turned five, when Vanessa decided to stay with the pack. You were beginning to ask questions, so we knew that if we were going to get you away from the mountain, I had to get you out of there."

The more he spoke, the more Lexi accepted the strange story. The thought of the sacrifice her parents had made to try to protect her, overwhelmed her. The knowledge that her dad had willingly left her mom and tried to make a good life for her... *did* make a wonderful life for her... made Lexi adore him even more. Panic hit her in the form of a burst of anguish. She thought of her father, returning to Sunchaser without her. "Dad, if I decide to stay, will you stay with me?" Her voice was barely a whisper. A part of her continued to feel as if the whole conversation was surreal, and yet now, she felt a strange sense of loss about leaving a place she couldn't even remember.

"I don't want to make that a bargaining chip in your decision, Lexi. I don't want to be responsible for making you suffer the way your mother did. Vanessa wouldn't want that, either." Jacob felt a fist grip his heart, when he added, "I don't want you trying to pull yourself away if I decide to leave and you can't. It almost killed your mom."

After another sip of coffee, he cleared his throat of emotion and continued. "Like I said, there's a little more to it. Lexi, you got yourself a mate up there that's waiting to meet you. See, usually the pack is raised together and everyone knows one another. Even so, until one of you starts shifting, you won't know who it is. My guess is that's why the dreams have begun to hit you. I think you've got a fella' waiting for you up there who's already a shifter, and it's drawing you back there. I was afraid it was that Brent character, but it's not. He's a shifter alright. He's a cougar, though."

Jacob tapped the side of his cup. "I wondered about that, and I figure your fella' wouldn't want another wolf around you and he called in a favor. The cougars tend to be a little better at communicating their thoughts. Wolves just tend to get straight to the point and barrel their way through the door... damn the consequences. At least your guy had the sense and foresight to send a cat."

Lexi opened her mouth to ask a question, and Jacob held up a hand. "Hold on a minute. It gets even better." Jacob reached out his empty cup. "Get me some more coffee, would you? I barely chewed a cup of my own muck down this morning." Jacob tried to stop adding grounds at the prescribed number of scoops, but the basket always looked too empty, so he added another... then another... until the brown granules were almost to the top. Even though he knew that it was going to turn out terrible, he just couldn't stop himself.

When Lexi returned, she asked, "It gets weirder than finding out my parents and I can turn into wolves? Oh yeah, and I've got a wolf-man waiting for me up on a mountain?" Her mind flickered to the man in her dream.

"My guess would be that he probably spends most of his time on one of the ranches. Caves aren't bad for camping once in a while, but not full-time. At least, not for me, but your mom always liked them better. I've become spoiled with the comforts of home too much."

Jacob ran his finger around the lip of his coffee cup, and finally decided to tell her the rest of it. "So, here's the other thing. Did you know Michelle was adopted?" he asked.

"Yes, her parents told her when she was ten." Lexi's eyes widened. "Oh gosh. You're not going to tell me she's a wolf, too." Her mouth dropped open.

Jacob shrugged. "My guess is cougar. Actually, half from what I can tell from tracing her mom. Angela's deceased and there's no father listed on the birth certificate." Jacob was mildly pleased with his discovery. As soon as he had caught a scent from her, he had spent money that was supposed to go for fencing to hire a detective to search for Michelle's real mother. He figured she would have to have been dead to have deserted her kitten, and because it was the right thing to do... heck, it was to insure their community's safety and secret... he decided he had better check it out.

For Michelle to go through the shifting alone, if she was going to, was not the way they did things. She would need the help of her own kind to guide her through it. Even with the report tucked safely away in his hidey-hole, Jacob hadn't been certain enough to send word back to the mountain, until he had seen Michelle's reaction to Brent, yesterday.

"You gotta' be kidding me. Does she know?" Lexi asked.

"I doubt it, if she hasn't mentioned anything to you. Peggy and Drew certainly don't have any idea. They thought the reason the two of you didn't date was because you were experimenting together." Jacob laughed, remembering the conversation with them. "Drew had his shotgun loaded to chase off the boys, and Michelle never caught interest in one."

"Seriously?" It never occurred to Lexi that her friendship with Michelle, and their solo dating status, would cause her parents to come to that conclusion. "I had no idea. They always seem so nice to me," she murmured.

Jacob thought of Peggy, and the kindness she had always shown to Lexi. He had thanked her many times for filling empty pockets a 'dad' didn't think of. "I don't think they gave it too much thought after we talked. Anyway, if the two of you have mates waiting for you up there, you'll never be truly happy with anyone else," Jacob explained.

"But, I thought you said some of them came down from the mountain and marry regular people."

"Yes, but only the shifters who have no mates." Jacob rubbed his thumb down the side of his cup. "There are accidents up there, like what happened to your grandpa. Some shifters can manage to dive into the work of rescuing the mustangs off the mountain, but others, the shifters tied closer to the original bloodlines, become despondent and go up into the higher cliffs to shift, and they never shift back."

"Gosh, you mean they stay animals forever?" This seemed impossible. "Why would anyone do that?"

"You can lose a little bit of the hurt that way, so for some, it's easier to just hide behind the animal. After too long, their spirit is more the shifted-form than the person they were, and they can't find their way back."

Lexi thought of cougars and wolves roaming through the mountains. "It seems so lonely." Lexi was silent for a moment, contemplating a life as a wolf running through the mountain forests. It was weird, but she could almost understand how free it would feel. "Do you think there's a guy up there for Michelle, too?"

"Oh, I think he's already found her," Jacob replied, not sounding too happy.

Lexi's eyes widened. "Brent? You think Brent is her guy?" She was intrigued and tried to search her memory for any indication from the cowboy. In a way, he was good-looking and he seemed nice enough, but she did not go all wonky over him the way Michelle had. Lexi had to admit, she had never seen her friend go off the deep end like that for a guy before.

"Well, he sure seemed taken with her and she wasn't pushing him away, so I guess we'll find out. Lexi, when I get to Montana, I'll explain to Brent that Michelle doesn't know anything about this. Let him tell her, please. You don't know enough about what's going on, and I don't like to get that involved with 'cat' business. If he is hers, he won't do anything to hurt her. The cats are as protective as we are about their mates. Too many are lost. He'll be careful with her, and she'll be fine."

Now that he had time to think about it, Jacob considered the restraint the man had shown. Brent had probably figured his mate was lost and had tried to accept the fact, fighting the compulsion and draw to lose himself as a cougar on the mountain. To have been searching for Lexi, and finding his own mate… yeah, Jacob had to admit, the cat had been cool about the whole thing.

Lexi's mind was reeling. She could picture Michelle's rolling eyes with the news that Jacob would join them, just when she had a chance with her cowboy. "How the heck am I going to explain that you're all of a sudden going on the trip with us?"

"Well, if I don't meet up with you until Montana, my guess is Michelle's going to be pretty happy you're stuck with me so she can focus on Brent," Jacob reasoned.

Laughing nervously, Lexi said, "It will be nice to get back in August and find out this was just one weird summer. I still don't think I believe this." She scrutinized her father's face and saw no signs of what he had shown her the night before. "Does it hurt when you change?" Lexi thought it sounded painful.

"Just our clothes," he chuckled. "You sorta' black out for a second while your shifting from one form to another, but you keep a little of the mentality of both with you. Now you know my secret for picking horses." He winked at her. "If they aren't skittish around a wolf, they're going to be pretty sound."

"Do you think that's why I'm not more freaked out about this? I mean, looking at it from a normal perspective, this is some crazy stuff."

"You've got a good dose of wolf in you waiting for you to accept it. Just look at your room and how you've filled it up with them. It might be something you've always wanted." He began to laugh softly. "You know, I was more worried about telling you this, then our talk on the birds and the bees."

"Gosh, Dad. I've been raised around breeding horses, since I visited Michelle's quarter horse ranch. I have to admit that by the time we got to birds and bees, it was a bit of a letdown." Her eyes scanned towards the book again. "I didn't understand too much about the Indian's connection."

Jacob nodded. "The Crow legends are confusing. They believed in mystical beings they called the Little People. They were supposed to live in the Pryor Mountains." He shrugged. "Maybe they did or even still do. *Our* history doesn't explain where we came from and the Crow don't talk about it. Their legends say the Little People were able to help the Indian shamans transcend or shift when they walked up to the mountains to fast and have visions."

"See, the Indians never had horses until the white man brought them over, and they were mesmerized by the beauty of them. The Crow used to steal them from white travelers and other tribes. They say the Spanish mustangs of the Pryor Mountains might have come from a raiding party against Lewis and Clarke. The Crow never captured the mountain mustangs, but they used them to breed their horses to. Other herds on the plains came up from Mexico, or ran wild when the ranches failed and they deserted the animals."

"The say that the Little People were vicious in their protection of the mountains, and they'd kill just about anyone trying to pass through them. Indian or white, they didn't give a damn, until they met the Crow. About the only thing these Little People did like, were the animals. They especially liked watching the horses running wild and free through the mountain valleys. According to some of the Indians, they say the Little People were responsible for creating us. The Crow made a pact to leave the shifters alone and keep their secret, as long as we looked after the mustangs."

"With the Crow backing us, we got the Pryor Mountain Range almost completely secured. We weren't so lucky with the ranges in Nevada, Colorado, Wyoming, and such. Shifters moved down from the mountains and seeded themselves in areas to take in the mustangs that were being mistreated."

"That's why we've always taken them in?" Lexi was beginning to understand why she felt so close to them.

"Yes, and I should have known you weren't letting loose of your ties to the mountain, by the way you took to them. You spend more time with the mustangs than the auction stock, and there isn't any money in it. Still, I'd take them in even if it wasn't part of the pact, and I know that Mac feels the same way."

"Mac?" Lexi's coffee almost spilled. "You can't be serious."

"Oh, yeah." Jacob's eyes took on a faraway gaze. "He and I had some times running when he was younger."

Her eyes narrowed suspiciously, and she looked him up and down. "How come I've never seen you change? I mean, apparently not since I was little. You must want to."

"I go hunting twice a year, don't I?" His face lit up with a smile.

"Yeah, but you take the truck, camping gear, and your rifle," she said.

"It doesn't mean I use them, Lexi," he chuckled.

She sat silent for a few minutes twirling her finger on the arm of the sofa. "I guess I'd better call Michelle and tell her the trip is still on. I'm going to have to make her believe I had to wear you down."

Jacob tightened his face in mock anger. "I'll scowl around her for a few days. That should convince her."

Lexi rose to get the phone, calling over her shoulder, "Okay. Just don't growl at her."

Chapter VII

Brent pulled his truck into the ranch at dusk to find Nicholas waiting on the porch. "Welcome back."

"Thanks, it's good to be home." Brent grabbed his bag from the truck.

"I appreciate the favor, Brent. I owe you one." Nicholas held the door and they walked into the house. "I'll get us a couple of drinks while you stash your things in the guestroom."

When Brent returned to the living room, he said, "You don't owe me a whole lot. That other gal that was with her…"

"Yes?" Nicholas handed Brent his drink.

"I can't stop thinking about her. Damn, Nicholas, I think she's my mate," Brent finished.

Nicholas looked up, surprised. "A cougar? I didn't know there were any that hadn't been found." He winced. "I'm sorry, I shouldn't have said that." He also didn't want to mention he had not bothered to call the cougar leader, Paul, to check on the possibility. Brent was sent to look for Lexi, not go catting around for himself.

"It's okay. I considered over the past couple of years, mine might have been trapped or shot," he admitted. "I don't think Michelle knows she's a shifter, though. I'm going to ask the elders how this could happen. To be my mate, she'd have to be traced back to our pack. I don't understand it either, but she'll be here this summer."

"I hope it's true, Brent. You deserve it," Nicholas toasted him. *Enough about the cougar, tell me about...*

"I guess you want to know about Lexi." Brent sat down. "She looks a lot like her mother, and she's one helluva' rider. She's been riding, training, and starting horses since she was twelve, and helping with the mustangs since she turned seven. Jacob's not too pleased about all this, but he knows he's going to have to let her go." He looked out towards the mountains. "I didn't tell him about Vanessa."

"She didn't want you to. I'll go up tomorrow and let her know what's going on. I don't want her trying to come down here and messing things up for me again." He watched Brent trying to curb his tongue over the cold remark, and tried to amend his blunder. "The trip would be too much. I'll let her know we'll bring Lexi to her when she understands the situation a little better."

* * * *

Jacob made arrangements to bring his horses to Mac's. He told him he might be gone as long as a month and Mac assured him he'd check on the ranch while he was gone.

Lexi worked the last group of auction horses and they sold for a three-thousand dollar profit. Jacob put half of it away for purchases when they returned... if they returned. Daisy-May had been transported to Amy's, and Lexi spent the past week riding over there and explaining how to work with her. Daisy-May seemed to take to the girl, and Lexi was confident she had made a good decision with her placement.

The old book sat on Lexi's nightstand and she read it every night. The dreams still interrupted her sleep, but they did not scare her quite so badly. They left her feeling bereft and yearning, and it bothered her that she could not remember what the man in them looked like. Reviewing her journal, she surmised he had long dark hair and gray-blue eyes, but his features remained a mystery.

Michelle surprised her with an early birthday present of new boots. She wanted Lexi to have time to break them in, and she told her she had something else to give her when they exchanged gifts. Michelle's mom insisted on a copy of their itinerary and made Michelle promise to call her often.

At last, the big day came and Peggy drove them to the airport. With tears in her eyes she hugged her daughter good-bye. "The next time I see you, you'll be an adult. When did that happen?"

"Oh Mom, stop it. The next time you see me, I'll still be your little girl... your little princess," she added, trying to ease her mom's uncertainty. Michelle kissed her mother on the cheek and she walked to the plane with Lexi, turning once to wave.

The flight was long with two layovers, and they reached Jackson Hole by late afternoon. The girls put their things away in the motel and strolled around looking into shop windows and staring at mountain views. After nothing but flat land in Florida, the jagged heights of the Teton Mountains were breathtaking. The girls had a quiet dinner and went to bed early. They were exhausted after the long flight, and for the first time in months, Lexi didn't dream.

Day two was Michelle's birthday and they spent it on the river, white water rafting. The experience was exhilarating and both of them loved it. More and more, they found their eyes traveling northeast towards Montana… gazing across the cliffs towards the Pryor Mountain range. As they were leaving the river, one of the guides filled them in on the various places they might like to visit. Mentally, the young women were already planning to shorten their stay in Wyoming.

The bars were open until two, so they decided to rest after dinner and walk into a lounge at midnight to celebrate the passing of the princess crown. The place they chose was not too busy on a Tuesday night, and the girls took a booth at the back and ordered rum and cokes. The waitress smiled at their IDs.

She returned a few minutes later with their drinks and two shots. "Happy birthday, ladies. The first round is on the house, so I wouldn't let the boss off cheap and I threw in a couple of shots." She spread coasters on the table, and whispered, "They're just butterscotch schnapps and cream liquor, so they aren't too strong." She stood again, and said, "Enjoy your stay in Wyoming. You're a long way from home."

"Thank you, the mountains are awesome," Michelle replied enthusiastically, and Lexi nodded in agreement.

"Yes, well try a couple of winters here." She leaned down again, and whispered, "The thought of your Florida beaches has me drooling." She laughed and wandered off to another table.

The girls picked up the shot glasses and stared at them. They certainly looked harmless, so they toasted. "Here's to making it to adulthood with no major complications." Michelle clinked and watched Lexi down the drink.

"Except the darn dreams," Lexi replied, and licked her lips as she placed the shot glass back onto the coaster.

Lexi always handed Michelle her present first, because her birthday had technically passed. She smiled at Michelle's expression as she unwrapped a carved wooden cougar with tiger stone gems for eyes. She gazed at it, turning it in her hand and rubbing the smooth surface of the figurine with her fingers. "It's beautiful, Lexi.

"I bought it from one of the booths at the large auction in April. It's hand carved by the Seminoles. I'm so happy you like it. I love the eyes." Lexi had never mentioned Michelle's fondness for the wildcats to Jacob, even when he told her about his suspicions about her heritage. She smiled as she watched her friend lightly caress the polished wood.

"Lexi, it's beautiful and I know exactly where I'm going to display it." Michelle's bedroom was as immersed in cougars as Lexi's was in wolves. Ironically, neither girl's parents were aware of the other's fixation.

Michelle's eyes sparkled while she held out a small wrapped box. Lexi removed the paper to find a velvet jewelry box. She looked nervously at Michelle. "We agreed."

Michelle rolled her eyes. "Just open it. I didn't go that much over, promise." Michelle still clutched the carving, but looked excitedly at the box in Lexi's hand.

As soon as they were old enough to buy their own presents for each other, they made an agreement not to spend more than twenty dollars. Lexi frowned at Michelle. "The boots cost five times our limit already."

Michelle planned her reply in advance. "Ten, but those were really just payment for breaking Midnight Blue from rearing. You never take money from me for training, and it's not right." She pointed to the jewelry box, as yet unopened. "That's your real present."

Lexi opened the lid, and inside laid a sterling silver disk. On one half was etched the head of a wolf and the other side was the head of a cougar. Rearing up over them were two horses. The disk was broken by a jagged line outlining the animals' profiles, and two silver chains were attached to the rings at the top.

Lexi turned it over in her palm, studying it. "Where on earth did you find this?"

"I got it at a new age store in Gainesville. They design them on a computer and a machine etches it and cuts it out. Isn't it neat? It's kind of like those 'friends forever' necklaces, but only we will know what they mean." Michelle's smile broadened. "You get the cougar to remember me, and I get the wolf."

"Michelle, girl, I am speechless." Lexi separated the two halves.

The two girls hugged and helped each other with their necklaces. After another round of rum and cokes and two more of the tasty shots, Lexi began to feel a little guilty about keeping the shifter secret from her best friend. She had no idea how to discuss it with Michelle, and she finally decided her father was probably right about letting someone else explain it to her. After all, she was still reeling with disbelief about her own situation.

The next three days they spent hiking through the lower part of Yellowstone, enjoying the hot springs, the wonderful smell of the crisp mountain air, and the total immersion in nature. They waited for Old Faithful to gush forth its acknowledgment of their presence, and drove north where they camped for a few days before driving on to Montana. So far, the vacation had been perfect and Lexi had not had a single dream.

As they meandered through the green foothills, Lexi finally told Michelle Jacob would be waiting for them. "You're kidding. I didn't think anything would get him off Sunchaser. Why did he come up here?" Michelle looked more concerned than irritated, and Lexi was relieved.

Lexi tried to keep her cheeks from getting red, and she felt her heart begin to race while her fists gripped the steering wheel. She hated lying to Michelle, and leaving out pieces of the truth was just as bad. "I think he was a little worried about us meeting up with those cowboys so far away from home. I'm all he's got, Michelle."

Michelle turned to face her and her eyes widened. "He's not going to be at their *ranch*, is he?" Lexi didn't answer, and Michelle moaned, "Oh god, please tell me he isn't going to be there."

"I don't know. He just said he was meeting me in Montana."

"I *so* do not want him going on the camping trip with us. While you chased your dream, I was hoping to be chasing mine… in the shape of a tall, blonde cowboy." Michelle's wistful smile caused Lexi to shake her head. "The last thing I need is him reporting to Mom or babysitting me with Brent."

"Dad wouldn't do that, and besides, I'll keep him busy," Lexi assured her.

They pulled into a rest area and Michelle dialed the ranch. It rang twice before a deep voice answered. "Hello?"

"Um, Brent?"

"No, this is Nicholas. Hold on a minute, he's right here."

Michelle sensed the mouthpiece of the phone being covered. She looked at Lexi and shrugged her shoulders. "Nicholas answered, and he's getting Brent."

A few moments later a soft voice said, "Michelle?"

She felt an unfamiliar twinge of excitement. *Damn, he's hot.* "Hi. I'm glad you remembered me." *Stupid... what a stupid thing to say.*

"Two ladies visiting from Florida to break up the doldrums of the ranch? Of course I remember. You ladies survived your birthdays, I take it?"

"We had a blast. Jackson Hole is great, Yellowstone amazing, and we got drenched rafting. We'll fill you in when we get there. Anyway, we just crossed into Montana about twenty miles back. Is it still alright with Nicholas if we come up?"

"Trust me, he's looking forward to meeting Lexi and you. Jacob has been filling us in on some remarkable childhood memories," he chuckled.

The blood drained from Michelle's face, and she asked, "Jacob's there?" Michelle and Lexi rolled their eyes and groaned in unison.

"Yep, he got here yesterday. Apparently, he plans to single-handedly keep you two safely herded," Brent laughed. His voice became quiet. "I warn you, Nicholas and I plan to give him a run of it." Brent stared across the living room, where Nicholas and Jacob had begun to argue again. It had been nonstop since Jacob arrived. Brent was distracted by the phone again.

Michelle could not remember the last time she actually giggled. "Well, give us the directions to crash your party."

Michelle scribbled the map on the back of the ranch business card. "Okay, that should be easy enough. We'll see you in about an hour. Say hi to Jacob, and tell him Lexi's been missing him something fierce."

Lexi shot her a frustrated look as she hung up. "Thanks a lot. You know, I should have called them to let them know Dad might be coming. I didn't think he'd go to their ranch. This is so embarrassing."

"Oh, I don't know. Brent made it sound like they were having fun. God only knows what stories Jacob has told them about us."

Lexi shook her head sadly. "About fifteen years' worth of the worst stuff he could remember to chase them off, I imagine."

They spent the hour drive reminiscing about all the horrible things they did together while they were growing up. At least, the things Jacob found out about. "Remember when we were playing dolls and Jenny gave you that hideous plastic horse," Lexi laughed.

"The damn thing looked like it had been half melted, and she really thought I would put my beloved doll on its back." Michelle shook her head in disbelief.

"Well, you didn't have to break its leg off," Lexi joked.

"I was trying to straighten it. Besides, you're the one who shot it," Michelle grinned.

The two girls smiled, remembering how Lexi shot a pebble at the deformed horse through a straw to put it out of its misery… or maybe theirs'. They held a solemn funeral, all dolls in attendance in full western gear, and buried it under a mango tree in Michelle's backyard where it lay to this day, undisturbed. They both said in unison, "Cowgirl humor," and cracked up laughing.

Just before sunset, they pulled into a dirt driveway flanked by two wooden poles with a beam branded Wolf Creek Ranch and suspended by chains high overhead. Lexi stared at the sign and shivered.

"This is it." Michelle stared at the endless expansive pastures in front of them. "My god, Lexi, it's huge. I bet it's bigger than my place." Michelle looked on either side of the driveway at the cattle grazing on thick green grass. "What we wouldn't give for pastures like that."

"No kidding. I bet our horses would go crazy out here," Lexi agreed.

They drove for about five minutes and finally saw the barn, corrals, and large log ranch house with a wraparound porch. Michelle's mouth dropped open as looked around the well-organized area. "Wow, nice."

Lexi recognized her father's burly form and shaggy gray hair from the distance. "Well damn, no reprieve. Jacob's sitting with them on the porch." She remembered Brent and could not see the third man, presumably Nicholas, clearly.

They pulled to a stop and Jacob jogged down the steps. "Hi honey, happy birthday."

"Thanks, Daddy. We had a great time."

"Happy birthday to you too, Michelle."

"Thanks, Jacob, it was awesome."

Brent stepped off the porch to greet them, and just as he was saying hello to Lexi, her nostrils flared slightly and she turned towards the scent. The other man walked out of the shadows and as he approached the group, the color drained out of Lexi's face and she collapsed.

Chapter VIII

Jacob groaned. Any question about Lexi's susceptibility to her heritage… and her mate… had just been answered. Nicholas ran towards the fainted girl, and as he reached down to pick her up, Jacob growled, "She's still my daughter. I'll take care of her."

Michelle was already kneeling by Lexi's side, and looking at the men in confusion. "I don't understand. She's been fine all day and never said anything about being sick. God, Jacob, is she going to be okay?"

Jacob grunted as he lifted his daughter and walked towards the house. "She'll be fine, Michelle. See if you can find a glass of water or juice for her." Jacob laid Lexi on the couch in front of the big river rock fireplace, and knelt by her side. When Nicholas tried to join him, Jacob told him again to back off.

While Michelle was getting Jacob the drink for Lexi she thought about the man, Nicholas, she surmised, and could almost understand her friend's reaction. The man was at least six foot three and built as solid as any man she had ever seen. Beneath his black cowboy hat, his dark hair skimmed his shoulders. And his eyes... at first they looked grayish-blue like Lexi's and Jacob's, but when he got closer, Michelle thought they were more of an icy blue. They were intense and piercing, and focused completely on Lexi. Michelle shivered and returned to the living room.

Lexi was beginning to shudder awake with Jacob kneeling by her side, and Brent and Nicholas standing a few feet away. Brent had a concerned expression, and Nicholas, *wow*. Somehow, Michelle thought he had a look on his face that was triumphant. At least, that is how it appeared to her. The whole situation and scene was confusing.

"Here, Jacob. How is she?" Michelle asked.

Before Jacob could answer her, Nicholas' deep voice said, "She's fine. She's home now."

Michelle felt an irrational and immediate dislike for the man. She had absolutely no idea what his reply meant, but just the fact that he would answer about Lexi's condition without even knowing her, made Michelle angry.

Brent could sense Michelle's agitation and he gave Nicholas an uneasy look, and whispered, "You'd better cool it. These ladies have no idea what's going on, and you're going to scare them off." In truth, he was having a hard time controlling himself around Michelle. They had forwarded Jacob's information to Paul yesterday, and were still waiting for an answer about her background. It didn't matter. He could tell she felt threatened and he wanted to get her out of there, before the real dogfight began.

"She's mine, Brent, and Jacob has no right to keep me from her," Nicholas replied. His fists and jaw were clenched while he tried to keep control of his fury. "He's already kept her away too long, and that's what's causing her problems. If he'd stayed up here with Vanessa, Lexi would know what's expected of her."

"*If*, Nicholas. But he didn't, and Lexi has been raised away from the pack since she was a child. From what he told us, she didn't know anything about this until a few weeks ago, and he's not sure she believes any of it. You better take it easy with her," Brent cautioned.

Brent felt the vibration of the growl and heard the warning coming from his friend. Nicholas was destined to be the wolf pack's new leader, and his alpha tendencies were surfacing more each year. With his mate found, the trait would increase to give him the strength and leadership qualities he needed. But, they also made him dangerous when he felt the need to be protective… like now.

"Calm down, Nicholas. Lexi isn't going anywhere and I'd say by her reaction to you, she understands you have some connection to her, even if she's unaware of what it is. I think maybe Jacob and Vanessa need to explain to her what is expected of her," Brent suggested.

Nicholas' eyes were fixed on Lexi, and he felt a consuming dislike towards Jacob for keeping them apart. Nicholas first shifted three years ago, and he sensed through Vanessa that her bloodline contained his mate. It had taken until last spring, when Vanessa was still recuperating from the gunshot wound, to finally get her to reveal where Jacob had taken their daughter.

Nicholas had spent months stewing over the unfairness to him, the male who would be their leader, to be denied his mate over their selfish decision. For Jacob to think he knew better how to protect the girl, had him seething with anger. If Vanessa had died before disclosing Jacob's location, he may never have found her. At least Nicholas had reasoned with his father on that decision. Silas made no secret that he wish Vanessa was dead, because he was still worried Jacob might try to reclaim his spot as rightful leader of the pack when he returned. If Vanessa was gone and Lexi was no longer his concern, he figured Jacob would either go back to Florida, or lose himself in the cliffs.

Nicholas didn't give a damn about his father's worries, he was so angry with Jacob for hiding his mate, he hadn't told him Vanessa had been shot and the wound poisoned. She never recovered fully, and her health had deteriorated to such a degree, it was obvious she wouldn't last much longer.

Even when Aaron finally approached his father to contact the Crow, Silas had refused to call on the shaman to heal her. A long standing shifter rule, one of the first recorded after the original shifters began to run to the Crow with petty problems and minor disagreements, was that it was only the leader of the packs that could contact the Indians for help. The shaman made Silas nervous, and he decided there was too great a chance the Indian's weird mojo magic might uncover the fact that Nicholas' had been the who shot Vanessa.

Nicholas continued to angrily pace the room, trying to refrain from ripping Jacob away from Lexi. *It would have served Jacob right if the she-wolf died before he got back here,* Nicholas thought. It was possible. His father had told him Vanessa was very weak, and she probably couldn't take the trip down the mountain. Nicholas despised both Vanessa and Jacob for keeping Lexi away.

Brent saw the steel gaze and the fists clenched at Nicholas' side and Jacob must have sensed it too, because he turned and quickly issued his own growl of warning. Brent chanced placing a hand on Nicholas' arm to hold him back. Thank god Michelle was focused on Lexi and missing the exchange.

As soon as Brent got word back from the cougar pack leader, Paul, he was going to get Michelle away from the dogfight so he could bring her to his mother and they could explain things to her. It was not that the cougars were less protective; they just seemed to have the knowledge that communication and understanding was the way to a more positive conclusion than this intimidating display. Paul was an expert at tracing bloodlines, and he had been working on tracing Michelle since Brent returned from Florida... and discovered Nicholas had not bothered to mention it.

Brent decided to try one more time. "Nicholas, she has been raised by Jacob for sixteen years. Even if she realizes the draw of the mating pull, she's not going to do anything that would hurt her father. She may even leave again, if she thinks that's what he wants. You can try to force her to stay, but that won't work out well in the long run. Just look at Jacob and Vanessa."

"This isn't any of your business, Brent. They took her away, and they knew she would have had a mate waiting for her up here."

"Yes," Brent agreed, "and if we're right and Michelle's mother left us to have her baby in the city to get away, it leaves me in the same situation. But, with both her parents dead, she's not going to have anyone but the cougars to explain it to her. At least Lexi has Jacob and Vanessa, and I don't think it's too smart to set him more against you. He's already upset her mate is the alpha destined to be leader, and you know how Vanessa feels," Brent whispered.

"Yes, we *all* know how Vanessa feels. She wanted it to be Aaron." He glared at Brent. "But, it's not. It's me. And they all better come to grips with it pretty damn fast."

Brent realized nothing he could say was going to get through to him. The conversations between Nicholas and Jacob had begun poorly, and nothing had improved over the course of the past two days. Nicholas had basically told Jacob that after stealing his mate, there was no way he was letting her leave again. Jacob was trying to convince him to let Lexi make her own decision. Nicholas seethed, dangerously close to shifting, and declared angrily that if Jacob had not taken Lexi away to build a new life away from the pack, there would be no decision to be made.

Add to that, Vanessa was still waiting by the caves to see her daughter and husband. Brent had convinced Aaron to keep her up there, because no one was sure she could survive the trip down. Things were going to be disrupted enough with Lexi's arrival and to have Aaron added to the mix, Vanessa might not survive the animosity of a full-blown wolf-fight over her daughter.

Aaron had been providing for Vanessa long before he discovered her daughter was also destined to be *his* mate. The bloodlines compelled the inherited link. Unfortunately, as he was the younger cub to Nicholas, his brother would claim her. As Aaron was not going to be able to provide for his mate, he opted for his next available chance for solace. He got some comfort and felt camaraderie with the opportunity to look after Lexi's mother, and from an external choice, it was the most he could do for his mate.

Vanessa had made no secret that she never liked Nicholas. Even for an alpha, he was far too dominating. As boys, the twins could not stop fighting. The scathing battles continued, escalating over the years, until Nicholas eventually moved to the ranch and Aaron stayed up by the caves to take care of her.

Nicholas had every intention of returning to the caves once he claimed his mate. Vanessa would die, Jacob would leave, and Aaron would permanently shift, tuck tail, and head for the hills. Nicholas despised the confines of working within the non-shifters' laws and he yearned for the freedom and strength of his wolf-form. Reluctantly, he admitted the struggle to search for Lexi was handled easier from the ranch.

Nicholas paced the floor, watching angrily as Lexi became conscious and hugged her father. This infuriated him further, and he shrugged off Brent's hand when he reached out to try to calm him down, glaring at Jacob.

Lexi released Jacob and slowly swiveled her head in Nicholas' direction. Her eyes widened, and she stared at him in mute silence for a minute before whispering, "Dad, I want to leave here." Lexi was terrified, but determined. The hatred Nicholas felt towards her father, wafted through the room in tense fury. Lexi could *smell* it.

She was also confused. Part of her was undeniably drawn to the big man, but a bigger part of her mind took one look at the fierce expression on his face and the anger consuming him, and it scared the hell out of her. She thought about what her father had told her before they left, and she looked at Jacob with wide eyes, filling with fear but beginning to pulse with indigo striations of warning. "Oh god, Daddy. That's not him, is it?"

Jacob placed both weathered hands on the sides of her face, and he stared into her eyes. He could see and feel her agitation. *She's close to shifting, and she has no idea what's happening to her.* He kissed her forehead. "I'll take care of this, Lexi." Jacob rose, and he turned to face Nicholas. He spread his feet, and said, "I'm taking Lexi up to see her mother."

"No, Jacob. You're not," Nicholas replied coldly.

The two men stared at each other, facing off with one prize in mind. Lexi rose and stood next to her father. Michelle joined her, trying to slide beside her without being noticed. She didn't realize Brent was completely focused on her, and he slowly made his way towards his mate. Waiting for Paul's formal declaration was mere protocol. Brent knew Michelle was his, and although a cougar would never stand a chance against a wolf Nicholas' size, he had to protect his mate if he felt she was threatened.

Lexi stared at her father and the stranger. *Nicholas? Her mate?* She saw the men's fists clenching, heard the rumbling growls, and despaired over the differences in size and age of the adversaries. This man could rip her father apart, and she had no doubt Jacob would not back down from protecting her. Lexi cautiously moved around Brent, facing Nicholas.

Her voice quivered, but she looked up at the man and as calmly as she could manage, she said, "It was a mistake for us to come here. I apologize for inconveniencing you and disrupting your home." Without letting her eyes drop from his angry stare, Lexi said, "Dad… Michelle… we're leaving. Now." The glare Nicholas returned was pure ice, and Lexi felt an unusual feeling coming over her… along with a self-confidence she could not take time to examine.

From behind them, Nicholas deep voice seemed to penetrate the surroundings, bouncing off the river-rock fireplace and echoing in Lexi's mind. "I don't think you will be leaving again, Lexi. Your father had no right to take you away."

Lexi was not fooled. She could sense, and almost taste, the rage just below the surface of his façade. She continued meeting his gaze. "Brent, please take Michelle outside."

"I'm not leaving here without you, Lexi. Come on, let's get out of here." Michelle was wide-eyed, and she also had a heightened sense of the fury in the room.

Brent took Michelle's hand and she turned to him. "Michelle, it probably is better if we wait outside. I can't explain it to you just yet, but we really shouldn't be here."

Michelle wanted to argue, but the look in the handsome cowboy's face convinced her to follow him. He was really worried about her, and she decided he must be able to gauge Nicholas' mood better than she could. Michelle glanced anxiously at her friend, but allowed Brent to lead her out to the front porch.

"Lexi, you need to go with Michelle," Jacob said, and he tried to grab her hand and place her behind him.

Lexi evaded his grasp and continued to stare at Nicholas. "I don't understand a lot about what is happening, but I do understand that I will not allow my father or myself to be threatened or bullied. I have not been raised by your rules, Nicholas. And I do not feel any obligation to abide by them."

Nicholas laughed, but there was a cruel viciousness in his eyes. "Not my rules, Lexi. Nature. You've seen your mate and your home, now." He folded his arms across his chest, and he snapped, "You can't leave any more than your mother could."

His confident, sneering tone made her furious, and Lexi turned and took Jacob's hand. She began walking towards the door, effectively dismissing the arrogant, angry man. She had walked barely three steps when she heard the growl, and it stopped her dead in her tracks, freezing her blood. The tone deepened, hitched, and bellowed, and Lexi turned to find herself standing a few feet away from the largest wolf she had ever seen. He was beautiful and dangerous, just as the wolves she had imagined and surrounded herself with since she was a child. The wolf drew back its lips and kept growling deep in his throat, daring her to take another step.

Lexi took a deep breath. "Screw you," she said clearly. Where she had gotten the nerve to stand through the unimaginable change from man to wolf, to look into his fierce eyes and defy him, she could never figure out. It pissed him off, though.

He advanced rapidly with the intention of batting Jacob out of the way. Before he made it to them, Jacob changed. Lexi was left with the surreal vision of her father as a large gray wolf, circling the bigger beast. Nicholas attacked and Jacob was quickly wedged underneath the larger wolf's body.

The younger animal tore into him with his razor sharp teeth. For the first time, Jacob felt the age in his once lean, sinewy muscles as they strained to roll the younger wolf over. In his submissive repose, belly exposed to Nicholas' swiping claws, he would soon be ripped to shreds and lying bleeding, helplessly dying in front of his daughter.

Jacob scrabbled his hind legs trying to reach the soft underbelly fur of the wolf on top of him. Nicholas leaned down, resting his ribcage so close to the old wolf, that Jacob knew he could feel his labored breathing. He could see the victory in Nicholas' piercing gaze. Jacob felt claws tear through his side, and he smelled the blood. Rising over the snarls and growling were the angry, piercing sounds of Lexi's screams.

Suddenly, Lexi's shrieks stopped, and a burning sensation tore through her for an instant, numbing her thoughts and clouding the horror of the battle in front of her. When she came out of the fugue state, Lexi found herself with her teeth tearing into the muzzle of the wolf attacking her father.

Her *teeth*? She glanced at her hands. *Her paws?* The part of her that wanted to shriek at what she had become was pushed below the surface, and her survival instincts kicked in to save her father. In a flurry of fur, snapping jaws, and swiping claws, she bit Nicholas' muzzle, clawing at his face trying to get to his eyes… and all the while Nicholas ripped into Jacob.

A brief flash of her dream mixed through the feral thoughts commanding her mind, and Lexi finally realized the only way to save her father. Opening her jaws, she let go of Nicholas, growled, and dove through the living room window. She bolted towards the tree line at the base of the mountains and listened to the howl from someplace behind her as she kept running.

Brent was holding Michelle against his chest. She began crying at the howls and horrible sounds coming from the house and twice he had to hold her back from trying to go inside to help Lexi. Michelle screamed when a wolf came crashing through the window, not four feet away from her. A few seconds later there was a heart wrenching howl, and a second wolf… a huge wolf… came bounding through the broken frame.

Michelle grabbed the railing, still screaming as the wolves ran toward the mountain. Brent sat her down on the steps, feeling his gut tighten with his mate's obvious fright. Worse, he could not risk telling her anything that could calm her fears. She was shaking and crying, while she called for Lexi. He tilted her chin and forced himself to remain calm as tears washed down her cheeks from her beautiful green eyes. In the calmest voice he could manage, he said, "Michelle, wait here for just a minute. Let me make sure it's okay to go back inside."

She gripped his sleeves. "Brent, what's happening? How did wolves get into the house? Oh my god, poor Lexi," she moaned.

Brent ran his thumbs down her cheeks and kissed her forehead. "Just wait here, Michelle. I'll be right back." Brent squeezed her shoulders and walked into the house to check Jacob. There was no doubt in his mind that Lexi and Nicholas were gone, and he was terrified about what was going to happen to the girl when Nicholas caught up to her.

His instincts were to protect his mate, so Brent knew that his first problem was Jacob. He was naked and curled up on the floor, bleeding from a multitude of bite marks and Nicholas' powerful slashing claws. Brent winced. Nicholas had meant to kill Jacob, and Brent hoped that if Lexi somehow managed to reach Vanessa, Aaron could protect them.

Brent wrapped a blanket around Jacob and carried him to the sofa. He walked out to the porch for Michelle, and tried his best to sound calm as he told her, "Michelle, one of the wolves got Jacob." She was staring towards the mountains, and the direction the wolves had run. Brent pulled her gently to her feet. "I need you to help me slow the bleeding, so we can take him and get help."

Michelle was still crying. "Where's Lexi? Did the wolves... oh god, where's Lexi?"

Brent guided her into the house. *What a mess.* "Nicholas must have gotten her out of the house. They aren't in here, Michelle. We'll have to find them later." She kept turning towards the mountain, and Brent gently took the shocked girl's chin and turned her so she focused on him. "We need to help Jacob, and then we'll go find Lexi. Nicholas won't hurt her."

Brent hoped he wasn't lying. No wolves could get along with Nicholas. Brent had known him growing up. As a cougar, he posed no threat to Nicholas' position in the pack, so both facets of shifters had convinced Brent to stay with the man and try to keep his wild nature pacified.

When they had discovered where Lexi was, Brent had truly hoped that she would receive Nicholas, and that having his mate would calm the wolf down. Now, Brent was left feeling guilty about bringing the young women here, even though he had found his own mate in the process. He watched the lovely blonde girl silently cry, as she rinsed the blood off of Jacob and her trembling hands managed to bandage his wounds.

Jacob was half-unconscious, and murmuring, "Lexi... Lexi run, baby. Lexi, find your mother."

Chapter IX

Lexi ran through the forest, scampering towards the trail with a determination she had never felt before. The speed of her mad dash was alarming at first, but quickly turned to a feeling of exhilaration and she did not consider she was running on four legs, instead of two.

She heard the crashing of the larger wolf chasing her, but Lexi was strong and her smaller size made it possible for her to duck under and between branches her adversary had to circumvent. Purposely racing through thickets and underbrush, she blazed a trail difficult for him to maneuver and follow.

Uppermost in her mind was the hope that Brent and Michelle could get her father to safety and see to his wounds. Her new paws became bruised on rocks and underbrush, but she barely registered the pain. Lexi knew she had to put distance between herself and the beast chasing her.

The strangest part was that it all felt so natural to her. The unusual new body was agile and comfortable. The fur coat was warm, rocks, though bruising, did not cut her feet, and when she inhaled she smelled scents she could not describe. Wonderful things that made her feel at peace with her surroundings… it was a feeling of coming home.

She reached the cliffs and barely hesitated as she leapt across wide gullies and crevices, making her way up the mountain. There was no logic for her decision to travel up the slope, but something inside her told her it was the right direction. If she had been in human form, she would have recognized the path from her dreams. Lexi was now running up Wooten's Trail.

Subconsciously, she scrambled up the all too familiar path from her dreams and bounded up the narrow trail. She turned once, thinking she sensed Nicholas gaining on her, and her feet slipped on loose rocks. In panic, she felt herself falling, and her paws scrambled futilely trying to gain purchase as she slid over the side. Stars flashed behind her eyes as her head hit, and there was a sharp burst of pain before she was mercifully rendered unconscious.

Nicholas howled his despair when he scented where his mate had gone over the side of the ravine. He saw the marks from the scrambling of her paws as she had tried to pull herself back up, and he listened and flared his nostrils. He caught the scent of her blood far below and howled again, shaking his shaggy head in anger. There was no sound of movement, and lifting his muzzle, he scented no breath. His mate lay broken and bleeding, dead at the bottom of the cliff. An angry howl burst from deep within him, causing birds to take flight and animals to freeze in their tracks.

Nicholas slowly turned back towards the ranch and his piercing blue eyes glared through the darkness. *Jacob. You have done this by taking her away from me.* He began padding slowly down the trail, increasing his speed until he ran maniacally through the trees, ignoring the frozen elk and deer trying to hide from his terrifying presence.

The closer he got to the ranch, the more fury filled him. *Jacob. If you had not taken her away, she would know her position in the pack. She would know her position as my mate.* Nicholas' rage consumed him, and he blamed both Jacob and Vanessa for the tragedy. His mate would have learned how to travel the mountain trails, if they had not deceived him by taking her away.

When he returned to the ranch, it took him a moment to realize the scent of Jacob's blood was old, and he changed form when he walked through the ranch house door. Nicholas' eyes swept the room, and all he found was the destruction surrounding him… and blood streaked on the sofa. Brent, Michelle, and Jacob were gone. Nicholas' hands shook and he poured a stiff drink, slammed it down his throat, and stormed towards the shower.

* * * *

Brent glanced at the seat beside him while he flipped open his phone. The truck bounced along the dirt road leading to the cougar leader's home. It was the longer path, but Brent thought cutting across the dips and hills of the pasture would cause Jacob more harm. If he was not in such bad shape, Brent never would consider bringing the wolf into the elder cougar's den.

Brent clenched his jaw, watching the panic in Michelle's eyes while she tried to staunch the bleeding, and he decided this was the only course open to him. He sure as hell was not bringing his mate to an angry wolf pack. "Paul? This is Brent." Brent's voice trembled, as he tried to tell the elder what transpired at the ranch. Luckily, Michelle was distracted and trying to tend Jacob's wounds, but Brent kept his message as cryptic as possible.

Paul's decisive voice calmed him. "Bring him here and we'll try to stitch him up."

"Are you sure? The dogs might not like us messing in their affairs." Brent glanced at Michelle after the slip, but she was crying quietly and whispering to Jacob.

"It was an unprovoked attack, and I'm calling in the Crow to negotiate if there looks like any repercussions." Paul hesitated a moment, and added softly, "You're right about the girl, Brent. I'm having Sophia come over."

Brent thought of his mother, Sophia, and her calm demeanor. She would be thrilled to know her son found his mate, even if she was only half-cougar. No one had known for sure why Angela had made the impulsive decision to leave the mountains, not even her father, Paul. Still, Angela had been respected when she had lived among them. "Thanks, Paul. With all this going on and her unaware, it might be best for mother to get her away from the conflict."

"What about Jacob's daughter?"

"She ran towards the mountain. I'm hoping Aaron senses her. There was no way to shift... um... leave Jacob." Brent felt like an idiot, and he kept staring at

Michelle to make sure she was not picking up his discussion.

Paul was silent for a moment, and he finally said, "I'll call Silas over. Something needs to be done, and they need to know Lexi might not be safe."

Brent closed his phone and tried to focus on the road. Silas, the wolf pack leader, made all the cougars nervous. It had become apparent he was trying to ease out the cougars' claims on the mountain. To have both the Crow protectors and leader of the wolves meeting had not happened in Brent's lifetime. There was no doubt that Nicholas would somehow cast blame on the cougars, and Brent was certain Silas would back him. Brent realized he had put Paul in a terrible position. He glanced down at Jacob's wan face. "How is he?"

Michelle's green eyes were filled with tears, and she was fighting for control. "The bleeding has slowed down, and his breathing isn't any worse." A soft sob of frustration and pain hitched in her throat. "I don't know what else to do."

Brent reached across Jacob and curled her hand into his. "You're doing fine, Michelle. We'll be someplace safe where Jacob will be taken care of in a few minutes."

"Brent, how did wolves get into Nicholas' house?" Her blonde ponytail swept her back while she shook her head in confusion. "I don't understand. And Lexi… where is she? She's got to be going crazy with worry over her dad."

Brent felt his chest tighten painfully with her distress. It was a feeling he had imagined, but now that it was real, he was in anguish and trying to figure out how to soothe her. "Lexi is fine, Michelle. Nicholas won't let anything happen to her." Brent gripped the wheel and mashed the pedal of the pickup, swerving on the dirt road towards his elder's ranch.

They arrived to find the house brightly lit and the opened door washing a yellow path across the yard. Brent recognized the burly shadow of Silas, standing next to Paul on the porch. An Indian leaned back against the railing, watching them in silence. Brent felt a measure of relief. He knew the Crow would use the knowledge of his tribe's legends and heritage to decide a fair accounting of the tragic events.

Silas bounded down the steps when the pickup pulled to a stop. After Michelle slid out of the seat, the big man reached in for Jacob. "Move it, kit-cat," he muttered.

Michelle shuffled aside, appearing not to consider his strange words. "Is he going to be alright?"

Silas turned to look at the girl. Tears washed down her cheeks, and he inhaled again making certain he had detected the faint cougar scent as her own, and not some of the disgusting musk transferred by the 'tom' escorting her. He looked up at Brent and saw him shake his head. *Ah, little kitty doesn't know? That explains her concern for the dog.* "He'll be fine, once we get him bandaged."

Michelle shivered and wrapped her arms around herself. "Lexi, his daughter, is somewhere outside by the ranch… where the wolves are."

Silas smiled at her worry. "She'll be fine. Nicholas won't let any harm come to her."

The tension and horror of the evening hit her all at once, and Michelle exploded. "Stop that. That's what Brent keeps saying. She's running around, probably lost with that brute. He's as bad as the wolves." She looked at the shadows on the porch. "Somebody needs to call the police."

Silas' eyes narrowed on the girl, and a fleeting memory of Angela's eyes condemning him, hit him full force. *It can't be.* Damn, Paul had been muttering some shit about a granddaughter, but Silas had ignored him. It wouldn't take much for them to trace her lines and discover her daddy was Angela's mate, and not some flatlander she'd met in the city. That gave Michelle the opportunity to reestablish the cougar's link to leadership. Silas figured he'd better handle the crisis with Jacob first… but, the girl would also have to be dealt with.

His eyes flashed, and he growled. Michelle cowered back against the side of the truck, and he snapped, "This is none of your business." He hoisted Jacob up and carried him into the house, leaving Michelle standing open-mouthed by the truck.

Sophia's car skidded to a halt and she ran up to her son. "Brent?"

"Silas is taking care of Jacob." He led her over to the other side of the truck. "Mom, this is Michelle." The feeling of relief loosened his stomach, now that his mate would finally be cared for.

Sophia smiled and curled a lose wisp of the girl's hair behind her ear. She was terrified and in pain over the evening's events, and Sophia realized the strain her son must be under at not being able to do more for her.

"You have Angela's eyes." She looked up at her son. "Has Paul seen her yet?"

"Mom…"

"I know, Brent. Paul explained it to me." Sophia felt overwhelming happiness that her son had found his mate. *How terrible for Paul to be dealing with wolf business, and not be able to rejoice and greet his granddaughter.* "I think Michelle and I will go to the kitchen and have some tea while things get straightened out."

Michelle looked into the kind green eyes, and she broke down. "We need to call the police or park rangers. My friend is outside, running from the wolves that hurt Jacob."

Sophia pulled her close and caressed her back. Her fingers stalled in surprise, when she felt the distinct vibration of a purr. "Lexi will be fine, Michelle. I know that isn't easy to understand, right now. Come inside and we'll talk."

For some reason, the woman's calm voice and touch reassured her. It was obvious none of these people were going to call the authorities, and Michelle left her cell-phone in her purse at the ranch. The woman put her arm around her shoulders and led her towards the house. Michelle whispered, "Who's Angela?" Too much was happening too fast. These people were strange, and she was beginning to regret the decision to follow Lexi's elusive dream.

Brent took her hand as they crossed the yard and she felt the serene peace of comfort wash through her. "There's a lot you need to be told, Michelle, and Mom would be better at explaining it to you." He led her up the steps to the porch and Michelle glanced at the silent Indian, still standing by the door.

"Iishbíia," he murmured, and smiled at Brent's nervous expression.

"You're sure?"

"She has the strong blood of her mother and father. I am sure," the Indian confirmed. He followed them inside, leaving them to wander to the kitchen while he checked on the injured cheéte.

Silas watched the Crow's wife tend to Jacob's wounds, applying a salve that had been handed down since the time of the Little People. It was a secret magic the Crow refused to share, though Silas had tried to get them to divulge the mystery. The elder wolf winced at the damage to Jacob's body. Silas had not seen Jacob since he left so many years ago, in his futile attempt to protect his daughter. It was good that he was back to spend Vanessa's final time with her before she passed. Besides, it was far too late for Jacob to try to regain his rightful position as pack leader. Of course, with Lexi back, the matter was settled, anyway.

* * * *

In the darkness under the ledge, Lexi's eyes slowly opened. She was naked and bruised, with blood seeping from a wound on her forehead. It took a moment for her thoughts to clear, and she peeked over the side to a black yawning crevice. "Oh god," she gasped, and crept back in terror against the wall.

"Lexi, can you hear me?"

The deep voice startled her as it echoed softly into the ravine. It sounded like Nicholas, but gentle, somehow. *It sounds like the man in my dreams.* She was terrified and didn't answer.

"Lexi, I can feel you're afraid." The man's voice was kind and quiet, and it reminded Lexi of her work with the mustangs. "It's alright now. Your mother is waiting for you. Let me help you." Aaron smelled the blood, but it was already slowing. More than that, he smelled her fear. It clenched his insides, making him feel like he had when Nicholas used to blindside him with a fist in his belly, when they were boys.

He was serving Vanessa dinner, when he scented the shifted girl running towards them. Her fear and the exhilaration of an uncertain first shift assaulted his senses. Abruptly, her approach stopped, and he heard Nicholas' howling wail. Panic seized Aaron's chest, and he wondered how badly his brother had hurt her. Oh, how he wanted to battle his twin and keep the girl safe. He fought to keep the anger out of his voice. "Lexi, reach your arm up. Trust me, I won't let you fall."

Lexi watched an arm reach down from the ledge, and a familiar strip of leather with a dangling bead was wrapped around the wrist. Tentatively, she reached up. The man did not tighten his grip until he felt her confidence, and she clutched tightly to his hand.

He pulled and she began frantically pushing herself up with her bare feet pressing against the rock, scrabbling for purchase and inching up closer to the top until she lay by her rescuer's boots. Aaron shrugged out of his coat and draped it around her shoulders, and then he helped her stand.

Lexi stared at him uneasily, remembering the eyes, the long dark hair… the face of the man in her dreams. "Nicholas?" This could not be the same man from the ranch; the man who brutalized her father. She had no feelings other than fear of *that* man.

Aaron mopped her wound with his kerchief and smiled. "I'm his younger twin, Aaron." Lexi looked down the trail, and Aaron said, "He's gone, Lexi." He had no idea why his brother would have left his mate, injured and barely conscious.

Lexi now realized who she had felt herself leaving behind. She shivered and tears spilled down her cheeks. "Dad." She explained the fight at the ranch, crying as she told the story of Nicholas ripping into her father.

Aaron wiped her tears and he was relieved to see his strength calmed her. "Brent would have taken Jacob to safety, and to get his wounds bandaged."

"But, he's a cougar." She looked up at Aaron, worried he would make fun of her.

"Brent *is* a cougar, and he is also a good friend. He's one of the few that can calm my brother, though the sight of you must have been too much." Aaron frowned. "I take it Nicholas wasn't too pleased to see Jacob?"

"He blamed him for taking me away," Lexi answered. She realized the man was leading her up the trail, and she looked behind them. Lexi half-expected to see Jacob standing on the trail, calling to her.

"He'll be fine, Lexi. Let me take you to Vanessa, and she'll tell us what to do."

Lexi scanned up the path, and she murmured, "I dreamed of you."

Aaron's hand tightened in hers. He wished it were true, but he knew it wasn't possible. In a sad voice, he replied, "No, Lexi. You dreamed of Nicholas."

"No, it was you. I dreamed of you helping me up the ledge, and of the leather strip on your wrist." She stopped and looked up at him. "Nicholas doesn't wear one, does he?"

Surprised, Aaron studied her closely, and then he held up his arm and turned the dangling bead. Inside was a small framed picture of Lexi from her graduation. "No. Jacob sent pictures and letters to Vanessa, and Nicholas never knew. She gave me this." Aaron shook his head. "But, you should only have dreams of your mate." This made no sense at all. Nicholas was the oldest, and Aaron had always known the sad truth that the mate would go to him. Aaron had spent years running through the hills and pastures, thinking about the future and life without a mate. He had battled through despair, racing through the cliffs and tempting himself to remain shifted, but he always came back. Aaron knew that he would, at least until after Vanessa's passing.

Lexi stated clearly, "I won't be with him, Aaron. I was afraid of him before he attacked Dad, and now…" Her voice lowered to a tone she barely recognized. "I'd tear out his eyes and throat if he came near me again."

Aaron heard the conviction in her voice. She was strong and proud, a combination that would never work for his brother until he broke her spirit.

Chapter X

The clearing was just as Lexi envisioned in her dreams. A wall of cliffs and caves lined one side, and in the center of the space sat a low fire encircled by rocks and occasional cut logs for seating. A frail woman with faded long auburn hair sat with her back to them, warming herself by the fire.

Aaron stood behind Lexi with his hands on her trembling shoulders. "It's alright. You're alright, now." His familiar whispered words sent a chill through her.

Somehow, her feet moved her forward. "Mom?"

The woman turned and Lexi held back her gasp. It was her mother, older and just as beautiful, but with a haunting frailness. "Lexi," she whispered, and tears coursed down her pale cheeks. "Thank you, Aaron."

"Vanessa, please don't tire yourself. She'll be here in the morning." Aaron had to force her to eat and rest, while she anticipated her daughter's arrival.

Vanessa looked over his shoulder. "Jacob?"

There was no easy way to break the news to her. "Nicholas attacked him. After I get you settled, I'll go check on him. I'm sure Brent got him to Paul's by now, and I scented Silas running down the mountain."

Vanessa nodded wearily, and turned back to her daughter. "Sit with me, Lexi."

Lexi sat down and took her mother's hand. "You're sick."

"Yes." Vanessa's weary gaze met her daughter's. "I was shot late last winter protecting the herd."

"You need a doctor." Lexi turned to Aaron in panic. "We need to get her help."

Vanessa reached for her daughter's hand. "Lexi, we can't go to doctors. Perhaps, if I'd known you'd come back, I might have gotten to the Crow in time. I've been too lonely up here without you and Jacob, but I wasn't going to chance calling you back. Not if it meant you could be safe away from the mountains." Vanessa looked down at their joined hands. "I decided it would be best to leave you alone, when I learned you belonged to Nicholas."

"Vanessa, she dreamed of *me*," Aaron answered.

174

Vanessa smiled sadly. "No Aaron, she would dream of the oldest. It is the way of the pack when there are twins."

"No, Mom." Lexi explained the ledge and the bracelet. "Michelle can tell you. She read it in my dream journal." Her cheeks reddened, and she said, "I felt nothing but panic and fear of Nicholas. I was trying to get Michelle and Dad to leave. That's why he attacked." She looked up at Aaron. "I don't feel that way with Aaron. I feel safe."

"Vanessa, Nicholas left her," Aaron said. The simple fact that his brother would do that, gave Aaron hope that perhaps Lexi was right. "Nicholas could not sense she was alive. How come *I* knew this, and he didn't?" Aaron felt miserable loss.

It didn't matter. If it was somehow true, and Lexi was his, Aaron would still have to cow to his older brother. Silas admired Nicholas' domineering manner and strength, and as pack leader, he would never agree to take Lexi away from his brother. As was the way of the pack, Lexi would have no voice in the matter.

"Aaron, take Lexi to my cave and get her something to wear." Vanessa laughed nervously and apologized. "We get rather accustomed to our natural state from shifting, though I imagine it will take you some getting used to."

Lexi followed him to a cave, and her eyes dropped to the ground. There was only packed dirt, and she knew that it wasn't the one from her dream. He showed her where Vanessa kept a small chest of clothing. "One of her skirts will work, but I'll get you one of my shirts." Lexi was a statuesque beauty, and Vanessa was smaller with a much frailer build.

Vanessa was stirring the ashes when they returned. Turning around at the sound of their footsteps, a tense fear filled her belly and she looked up at Aaron. He took her hands and stared into her eyes. Aaron knew that Vanessa could sense her mate's pain, and the distress would wear her down. He smiled and said, "I'll check on Jacob."

He could see the relief in her eyes, but she warned, "Nicholas might be there."

"He thinks Lexi's dead, so he won't be searching her out for a while. Visit with your daughter, and I'll bring back news as soon as I can." Aaron walked towards his cave and Lexi ran after him.

"I want to go with you." A part of her wanted to stay with the mother she had missed and longed for, but a bigger piece of her heart lay with Jacob and the threat Nicholas presented.

Aaron smiled. "You can't. You don't know how to shift, and I need to hurry."

"But, I did shift," Lexi reminded him.

Aaron chuckled softly. "Yes, but you were scared and fighting for Jacob. It will be a while before you can do it at will." Aaron placed his hands on her shoulders and stared into her gray eyes. Indigo threaded through them. It was an inherited trait from her mother and father and a sign of strength. Aaron's mind flashed on scenes of them shifting together, running up the mountain to the valleys. He shook himself free of the impossible reverie, and said, "It will all work out, Lexi. I'll get you away from here, before I'll see you saddled with Nicholas."

Lexi laid her head on his chest. She had never felt the feelings flowing through her that Aaron provoked inside of her. The uneasy realization occurred to her, that she had never truly felt safe and whole until she met this man. Not even at Sunchaser Ranch with her father and the horses. The feeling had been an immediate response, as soon as Aaron had pulled her up from the ledge. As was the way with the chéete, Lexi experienced the inherited trait of devotion and trust for her mate. "Mom is really sick, isn't she?"

"Yes, Lexi. I managed to get the bullet out of her leg, but she'd lost a lot of blood. It was infected for over a month, but she refused to let me send for a Crow healer." Aaron did not mention that his imploring requests to Silas had fallen on deaf ears. Once he had learned where Jacob and Lexi were, he discarded any thoughts of the injured she-wolf. Silas considered Vanessa passed prime, a solitary with no mate, and a drain on the pack's resources.

Aaron stroked down Lexi's auburn hair, wishing she could belong to him. "Mostly, I think Vanessa just didn't want to live anymore without you and Jacob. She was afraid for you when she learned you belonged to Nicholas. Silas, our elder, made her tell him where you were. He said Nicholas had to have his mate to settle him down, but no one believed it would work. She still wouldn't have told them, but she feared they would start following me and find out about Jacob's letters. Your mom needed those letters to know you were still safe. In the end, she hoped it would be wiser to give into Silas' demands."

Lexi walked back to the fire to sit with her mother. A few minutes later, a large wolf joined them. Vanessa smiled and stroked its head. "Be safe, Aaron. Don't challenge Nicholas. He'll be in a rage over Lexi." The wolf nodded and bounded down the path.

* * * *

Sophia tried to figure out how to explain the situation to Michelle. The young woman kept passing uneasy glances towards the living room, where Jacob was being tended by the Indian woman. "So, Angela is my real mother. Who's my father?"

"We don't know, honey. He wasn't from here." Sophia looked over at her son and saw the brief flash in his eyes. Oh, they had their suspicions, but that was all they were. There was nothing they could prove and bring to the Crow for judgment.

Brent sat on a chair next to Michelle, watching her closely and staring into her green eyes. She was the most beautiful woman he had ever seen, and he longed to watch her lithe cougar form run through the green mountain valleys. "Mom, the Crow said she was pureblood."

Sophia's smile froze. Now that the Indian confirmed their doubts, she tried to hide her shock, and murmured, "That's why Angela left." Sophia glanced at her son. "Does Paul know?"

"I don't think so. This is going to make things uncomfortable." Brent did not want to voice the thought that another all-out battle might take place in front of Michelle.

Michelle felt disoriented again. Everything that had happened, and most of what had been said, seemed confusing and surreal. "Pureblood what?"

Nicholas barged in through the door, and Silas and the Indian formed a wall with their bodies, keeping him from Jacob. The Crow remained silent, but Silas said, "Calm down, Nicholas. You had no right to take your frustrations out on Jacob. By all rights, he has as much authority as an elder."

"An elder?" Nicholas spat. "He gave up our ways for the flatlands."

Silas felt his stomach sour, and he was certain the Crow could tell something was very wrong. The Indians had an uncanny ability to read through the wolves' deception, and Silas was sure the Crow could hear the insincerity in his words. Silas had no choice, so he continued to try to control Nicholas before they were called for judgment. "Jacob never gave up our ways. He has spent his life devoted to protecting the herd."

"The horses? They are a dying breed and useless. No one wants them. Even the Indians have given up on them, and let them roam aimlessly through the mountains."

A stern voice condemned Nicholas' remark. "I am Native American. I am Crow." The shaman's tribe preferred to keep the name Apsaalooke among themselves, and used their white name when around outsiders.

Shocked, Silas looked up at the man. Only the cheéte and iishbíia could call them Indian, without it being an insult. Their history together and bond with the Little People, made this so. For the Crow to revoke this right from Nicholas, to outwardly voice it was an insult for the future wolf pack leader to call him Indian, was a very bad sign. Silas could not hold back his growl of warning. *Shut up before it blows up in your face. I'll deny everything.*

The Indian narrowed his eyes on Nicholas. "Careful, cheéte. You are safe only as long as you protect the iichíile."

Nicholas tried to push passed the Indian. "Crazy stories and legends."

More than anyone else, the shaman knew only too well, the truth of their history. "It is these crazy legends that have made you cheéte," the Crow reminded him.

"It is these crazy legends that have killed my mate," Nicholas snapped.

Brent gripped Michelle's arm, and she gasped, "He isn't talking about Lexi, is he?" Before they could stop her, she tore from Brent's grip and ran to Nicholas, screaming, "Where is she? What did you do to her?"

Nicholas curled his lip and spat, "Get away from me, cat. This isn't any of your business."

Michelle stepped back and straightened. She did not flinch from the steal glare in his eyes, and she hissed, "The hell it isn't, wolf-man." An amber glow lit through her emerald eyes and with a quick cracking of bones, a beautiful golden cougar stood in her place... a very angry cougar.

"She knew," Sophia whispered. The cougar looked back at her and smiled, her amber eyes shot through with brilliant emerald green. Brent reached for his mother's hand to steady himself. His eyes roamed the strong graceful figure and golden fur of the beautiful cougar, and he felt a sense of pride in her courage and loyalty towards her friend that was overwhelming.

Michelle had first changed the week after Lexi began having the dreams. She knew that somehow everything was tied together. It seemed her friend was unaware of the situation, and with cat stealth and patience, Michelle waited for Lexi to discover the truth.

Of course, she also had a lot of fun running through the back pasture away from the cows, learning to trust her new senses and agility. Sneaking back to the barn for her clothes, Michelle carefully scrubbed away signs of her paws' prints. *Lexi.* Michelle turned back to the wolf and hissed and snarled.

"Brent, you better get your spitting cat away from me," Nicholas warned.

Instead, Brent rose and stood beside the cougar. In a calm voice, he asked, "Where is she, Nicholas? Where is Lexi?" With a room full of witnesses, he still expected Nicholas to lie. He was not disappointed.

"She stumbled going up the trail." Nicholas bellowed into the other room, hoping the wounded man would overhear. "He took her away from the mountains, and she never learned the paths."

Brent shook his head, sadly considering the vast emotional disparity between Nicholas and his younger brother. *What kind of leader would blame his own folly that led to the death of his mate, on her injured father?* If only Aaron had been born the first cub, and able to claim the elder position for the wolves. Brent looked into Nicholas' cagey stare. His icy blue eyes were bereft of compassion, and filled with an arrogant fierceness that reeked of misguided power.

Brent had always played the role of liaison for Nicholas' unruly, crass behavior. Not this time. Not with Michelle, new to her cougar heritage, standing up to the wolf and making him accountable for his actions. Brent stroked down her back and he felt her quiver. "You're lying. I watched her run, Nicholas. She was steady and fleet-footed, racing to lure you away from her father." Brent sealed his lips when Paul gave him a look of disapproval. This was wolf business, but Michelle's close friendship with Lexi, complicated things.

Silas' expression was concerned and uneasy. With such an open accusation, it had to be addressed. "She tried to get away from you? Why would your mate do that, Nicholas? Lexi should be instinctively drawn to your protection and companionship." This certainly threw a wrench into the works. All Nicholas had to do was assert his rightful place as the girl's mate to claim leadership.

Michelle snarled, and Brent repeated his assessment of the situation at the ranch. "Lexi wanted to get away from him as soon as they arrived. She was trying to get Jacob and Michelle to leave with her, when Nicholas attacked."

Silas winced and glanced at the Crow. The Indian's expression did not change, but his dark eyes were staring intensely at Nicholas as he considered the cougar's words. *Lexi wanted to leave before her father had been attacked? A true mate would never be able to suggest such a thing.*

"Brent, take Michelle back to the kitchen and try to calm her down," Paul said quietly. Despite their involvement, this was wolves' business, and it was wiser to let them deal with their own mess.

Brent felt the vibration of Michelle's anger quiver down her spine. He knew that despite the odds, he would fight the wolf alongside her, if that was what she wanted. "Where is Lexi?" Brent persisted.

"She fell over the ledge, into the ravine," Nicholas thundered.

A ripping tear pulled through Nicholas' chest, but it was not a sense of loss for his mate. It was Michelle's claws. Nicholas watched his blood drip from the end of her paw, and he reached out and snapped her foreleg. She hissed and screamed in furious pain, lifting the limb off the floor.

Brent wavered between shifting, fighting the bending of his bones, and curling his half-claws into his fists. Things were out of control, and he tried to focus on his wounded mate. The Indian looked down at the cougar with a sudden kind pride in his piercing dark eyes. His voice was calm, and his quiet words resonated through the room. "Remember her dream, iishbíia. Remember the cheéte's dream."

Chapter XI

Paul struggled to control his own confusion and anger. Nicholas knew damn well Michelle was his granddaughter, and new to their ways. He steeled his resolve to remain calm when he had seen her shift. She looked so much like Angela, with the same unique eyes, and Paul felt the loss of his daughter all over again. Fighting his personal feelings, Paul sensed things were getting out of hand, and he looked up at the Crow for guidance. The Indian continued to take in the confusion, remaining silent, but obviously pleased with Michelle's defense of her friend.

Michelle fought the pain and the desire to claw the wolf to pieces. She limped back into the kitchen, favoring her injured front leg. There would be no use trying to fight Nicholas until she healed, though she vowed not to forget or forgive his abuse of both her and Lexi. Michelle transformed back into an angry young woman, holding her broken arm.

Sophia wrapped her coat around Michelle and studied the break. "Paul, I need the splinting kit," she called through the doorway, in a voice far calmer than she felt.

There was a knock on the door and Brent walked to hallway to answer it. After tugging on the jeans Brent handed him, Aaron passed by without explanation. The Indian moved to let him go to Jacob.

"Who's that?" Michelle asked.

"Aaron, Nicholas' younger brother," Sophia answered, concentrating on the task of wrapping the injured arm. She felt such pride with the girl, even if she did not understand that cougars played more of a background position in their society. Sophia smiled up at Michelle. "We were trying to figure out how to tell you that you were one of us." She rubbed her hand along the damaged limb. "You'll heal quickly, within a week. Keep it protected, but it's why we don't bother with casts."

Michelle watched Sophia work on her arm. "I was going nuts trying to figure out how to tell Lexi. When she began to have the dreams, the place she described was so familiar, that I decided to see where it led."

"The dreams," Sophia murmured. She looked into the girl's eyes, and asked, "Michelle, what did the Crow mean?"

"Lexi had dreams of being chased up the mountain trail." Michelle stopped speaking, and her eyes widened. She whispered, "Sophia, she saw herself falling over a ledge, and a man helping her up." Michelle glanced towards the other room. "She's alright. That man, the brother, he saved her."

Brent overheard the conversation, and he leaned down and whispered, "Keep this to yourself, Michelle. If what you say is true, Lexi is probably with Vanessa, and we don't need Nicholas to know until this is straightened out."

Everything inside her, knew this was true. Michelle was sure she would feel an empty, fathomless hole in her heart, if Lexi were truly dead. She nodded and sat quietly until Aaron left Jacob's side. Nicholas was already healing from Michelle's light swipe through his chest, and he glared at his brother. "Why are you here?"

"Vanessa sensed her mate's pain, and she asked me to check on him." Aaron shook his head sadly, and he looked back towards Jacob. "How could you do such a thing?"

"You question me, Aaron? I am the oldest. You have no right."

"You are alpha, Nicholas, as is your brother," Silas reminded him.

"I am firstborn. The leader."

"You forget yourself, Nicholas." Silas watched him shimmer in anger. "You are not the leader. I am. Or do you wish to challenge me, now?"

Silas was finally forced to admit, Nicholas did not possess the control to lead the pack. Worse, the wolf had disrespected their Crow protectors by denouncing their obligations to the mustangs, as well as causing a fracture in their precarious relationship with the cats. *And after Paul welcomed them into his home to help Jacob?* The Indians would see this as a serious breach in protocol, and Silas wondered if it was too late to back out of his partnership with his son. He didn't want to get caught up in things, if Nicholas lost his temper and divulged what they had been up to.

Nicholas watched Michelle's eyes train on Aaron's bracelet. She had calmed too much from her earlier display, and he remembered what the Indian had said to her. "What dreams did she have of me?" Nicholas demanded. He was certain his reputation would be redeemed, when the cat spoke of his mate's visions of pride and respect for his strength.

Michelle smiled with cat-like satisfaction, practically licking her lips. "She didn't dream of you at all, Nicholas." She pointed a finger on the hand of her good arm at Aaron. "It was him."

"You lie." Nicholas charged at the girl in outrage. Brent quickly positioned himself in front of her, and Aaron and Silas growled at his back. "I am the oldest. I am the leader."

The Crow shook his head. "No, cheéte. You are far too wild and dangerous to your pack and our ways."

Nicholas growled, "And what do we need *your* preposterous protection for? What good have your stories done us? To leave the mountains, we are slave to the horses, and staying here isn't safe. You are supposed to protect us. Vanessa was shot on the prairie last spring."

"Vanessa was shot?"

Heads turned at the sound of Jacob's weak voice. Michelle pushed between Silas and the Indian. She burst into tears and laid her head on his chest. "Oh god, Jacob. I was so scared for you."

The Crow woman smiled in approval at the girl and the sentiment in the injured man's eyes. It was good to see the iishbíia and cheéte together in peace.

"You stop your cryin', girl. Take more than a brat cub wolf to get me down." Jacob looked up at Aaron. "You didn't tell me."

"She begged me not to, Jacob. When you wrote to tell her about the dreams, she rallied enough to see Lexi again." Aaron could not bear to tell him the true condition of his mate. Vanessa might make it through the fall, but never another winter in the caves.

Nicholas watched his brother carefully, and the truth dawned on him. "You knew where they were?" Fur began encroaching on his jowls, and Silas placed a warning hand on Nicholas' arm. "All this time, and you knew where they were hiding?"

"I've been bringing Vanessa letters and mailing her replies for many years. She couldn't risk getting caught, but she was sinking into despair and shifting back from wolf-form less often." Aaron shrugged. "I knew what it was like to be without a mate, and I asked her to let me help her. I think it kept us both from succumbing to the freedom of remaining shifted."

Nicholas' nostrils flared, and he reached out and grabbed Aaron's hand and inhaled the familiar scent. His howl wafted through the room. It still echoed when he shifted and bounded out the door.

Chaos erupted, with Jacob trying to rise, and the Indian woman and Michelle holding him down. "Please, you can't do her any good if you don't heal." Michelle was frustrated with her own injury, and she looked helplessly at Brent. Aaron was already gone, running after his brother. Michelle nodded, and convincing herself she was strong enough, she stood and said calmly, "I'll go myself."

"This isn't cat business," Silas' cold voice reminded her.

"Yes. That stupid prejudice is what caused this mess." Michelle looked at the two factions, with Paul standing nervously to the side and Silas' furious countenance. She stared at the wolf leader. "What happened, here? Lexi and I have always been the closest of friends away from your world. And Paul didn't hesitate to bring Jacob into his home. He didn't hesitate to let *all* of the wolves gather here, not even Nicholas… and it isn't a sign of weakness or fear of you. He wanted to help."

"It is a sign of strength, trust, and friendship," the Indian agreed. "Together, you died at the white man's gun. And together, you were transformed into spirit beings. These petty disputes surfaced gradually, until we have cheéte like Nicholas in line to be leader. He has lost his compass of morality and judgment."

Silas sighed, half in defeat and half with the weariness of understanding he had chosen the wrong son to side with. It was obviously imperative for him to find a way to completely detach himself from Nicholas. "I need to get to Vanessa and Lexi. I'm sorry, but in Nicholas' rage it would not be safe for the cougars." Silas felt his house of cards begin to tumble. If Lexi did not take Nicholas as her mate, he would not be the leader and take Silas' place. This would most likely infuriate Nicholas, until he made the mistake of truly killing her this time, and exposing them both.

Michelle stiffened, and Jacob said, "He's right, Michelle. The cougar holds a proud place in the mountains, but it is not between two male wolves fighting over their mate."

"But, Jacob…"

"No, Michelle. Silas will send word to us." Jacob closed his eyes, praying both Vanessa and Lexi would be safe. The Crow woman looked at her husband and nodded. The shaman would shift and fly to watch over the conflict on the mountain.

Silas transformed into a silver wolf. He was obviously old, but he carried such an air of authority, Michelle searched nervously for Brent. The Indian followed Silas onto the porch, and as the wolf ran towards Wooten's Trail, the cougars, Jacob, and the Indian woman, began a lengthy vigil.

Nicholas' fury caused him to disregard his brother's chase. Aaron had never confronted him, and Nicholas was confident he knew his place as second born.

Aaron raced up the path. He scented the musky coat of Silas behind him, running at a steady pace. The shadow of a bird flying through the moonlit sky overhead, made Aaron quicken his pace. If Nicholas reached the clearing first and hurt Vanessa, it may be enough to cost them the Crows' protection.

Lexi had spent the past hour, speaking with her mother and learning about her wolf heritage. She lifted her head and tilted it to the side. "It's Nicholas," she whispered, both amused and frightened she could know such a thing.

"Aaron and Silas are behind him," Vanessa replied. She shivered, even though the fire blazed close to them. "I feel Nicholas' anger."

Lexi stood and she began to unbutton her shirt. "I think I see why you don't bother with many clothes up here."

Vanessa reached up and gripped her arm. "You don't know that you'll shift."

Lexi shrugged. "Then maybe the sight of me standing in my birthday suit will stop him." She smiled down at her mother. "I did shift last time, and I'm not feeling more cordial towards his advances now." She dropped the skirt and stood in Aaron's unbuttoned shirt, hanging almost to her knees.

Nicholas leapt into the clearing and stopped a few feet away from the women. He shook and stretched back to human form, gazing in cold fury at Lexi. "You dare humiliate me by this treachery?"

Lexi stared calmly back at him. "Which part, Nicholas? Getting you away before you ripped my dad apart? Or when you left me for dead on the ledge?" She walked away from her mother and continued the dangerous game of taunting him. "I'm not yours, Nicholas. You know that. I belong to your brother."

"No. Twins have only one mate, and she belongs to the oldest."

"Is this some convenient rule you invented? How could I ever forgive you for what you've done to my father?"

Nicholas wandered closer to the fire, and Lexi watched her mother. *Run. Oh god, Mom. Run.* Her plan to distract Nicholas had worked with her dad, but he was not going to be drawn away from her mom. It had not taken him long to figure out that her parents were her weakness.

"You have left injury with your games, Lexi; first your father, and then the cat. Will you be so selfish as to see your mother hurt?"

Lexi narrowed her eyes. "Michelle? You've hurt Michelle?"

"Just a snapped leg," he shrugged. "It's nothing that won't heal and have her mindlessly pouncing again, soon."

Vanessa summoned her strength to shift. If she did not run, Nicholas would use her to get to her daughter. She managed to barely harness the energy, and she knew it would be hours before she could change back. Nicholas' attention was drawn to Aaron bounding into the clearing, with Silas close behind him. From the corner of his eye he saw Vanessa preparing to leap into the safety of the woods. He grabbed her by the scruff of her neck, wrapping his hand around her throat. "I don't think so. You've made me suffer long enough to gain my mate."

Silas shook out of his wolf form. "Release her, Nicholas," he demanded.

"Or what, old man? Your time has passed. Leadership never truly belonged to you, anyway. If Jacob had not run like a coward…"

"Let go of my mother," Lexi said quietly. Vanessa was going limp with her struggle to stay on her hind legs. "You're no leader, Nicholas. No matter how you bully and threaten, you are no leader."

Nicholas kept his hand on Vanessa, but he lowered her so her front paws could rest on the log she had been sitting on. His icy blue eyes fixed on Lexi, and he smiled. "You don't know?"

Lexi glanced nervously at Aaron, and returned her focus towards her mother and Nicholas. "Know what?"

"Of course." Nicholas eyes held humor that bridged on insanity, given the circumstances. "They've kept you blinded in ignorance."

"Nicholas…" Aaron warned.

Nicholas turned towards his brother. "Oh, you failed to mention this while you were plotting to steal my mate and position?" He smiled back at the girl and tightened his grip around Vanessa's throat, again.

Nicholas' eyes narrowed on Aaron, and he felt a supreme, victorious triumph as his little brother's attempts at stealing leadership dissolved. "It is the mother's bloodline that determines the leader, Lexi. If you had been male, you would have been leader. Now, the honor is left to your mate." He chuckled at her uncertainty. "Your father took the link to our true heritage down to that ranch in the swamplands. And now, you figure Aaron wants you for your inept ability as a shifter? At least, I make no lies as to your worth."

"That's not true, Lexi." Aaron could not believe his brother would suggest such a thing.

"I know it's not, Aaron. Your brother is rabid with power, and that is the only draw he ever felt towards me." She watched him lift Vanessa's paws off the log. Her mother's tongue began to loll out of her mouth, and Lexi was getting scared. She had seen Nicholas' strength, and the frightening gaze in his eyes left little room to negotiate.

From a branch in the tree the bird watched it all, silently recording what he must tell the tribe. Their circle of protection for the wild mustangs was breaking, and it saddened his heart.

In the distance, high above them, a wolf called through the night… and Lexi knew what she must do. She would run to the hills as a wolf, taking the enticing lure of leadership for the pack with her, and never look back. Her eyes filled with tears, but she knew this was the only way to curb Nicholas' dangerously obsessive ambition. "Good-bye, Mom. Take care of Daddy." She issued a sound that was a cross between a laugh and a sob. "And don't let him make the coffee."

Vanessa let out a strangled yowl as she realized her daughter's intentions. She snapped weakly… uselessly… at Nicholas' hand.

Lexi gave Aaron one last look of longing, wishing she could feel the comfortable companionship he offered. The only way her parents would be safe and she could be free from Nicholas, was to run. She would remain a wolf and deny Nicholas the bloodline to make him the leader.

Aaron's eyes widened. Silas gripped his forearm, and whispered, "Let her go. We'd never get close to Vanessa, before Nicholas snaps her neck. You can scent her out and find her again." Silas counted on Nicholas breaking Vanessa's neck, as soon as Lexi bolted. The Crow would pass judgment and either banish or destroy him, and Silas' secret would be kept safe.

Aaron could sense his mate's decision, and it tore through his chest. "But, she's going to the land of the Little People," he argued. The shifters did not return from there.

"Then, we will trust they will protect her," Silas answered.

There was a screeching caw from the branch overhead, distracting Nicholas just long enough for Lexi to shift and bolt into the shadows. He turned back at the sound of branches snapping back after she passed into the forest, and he looked at the shirt lying discarded on the ground where Lexi had been standing a moment before. "No," he bellowed, and he tossed Vanessa to the ground.

Silas ran to her while Aaron shifted and leaped at his brother. He scored down his face before Nicholas had time to shift. Aaron fought ferociously to give Lexi time to escape. While his brother's strength came from an insatiable desire for power, Aaron's came from an innate, fierce desire to protect his mate.

By the time they parted, panting and whipping spit as they shook their heads, the brothers were covered with deep gouges and bite marks. Silas laid Vanessa's head in his lap by the fire, waiting for her to gain the strength to shift back to human form. It had been several months since he had seen her, and he was surprised at how weak she had become. It would have been so easy for Nicholas to snap her neck and end her useless existence for the pack.

The Crow remained on the branch over-head, and Silas had no chance to do the deed himself. The fighting wolves lay stretched on the grass in exhaustion. Overhead, the bird finally rose in flight, studying the path the girl fled, before flying back down to the plains.

Chapter XII

Lexi ran until her lungs felt as though they would burst from the chilled night air. Her fur coat kept her warm and she tried to focus on her path and not think about all she was leaving behind. Lifting her muzzle, she could smell no other wolves, and she stifled a longing howl of loneliness. It would be some time before she recognized the scent of other animals.

She wandered aimlessly; always up towards the summit, trying to figure out what to do. It was difficult to concentrate, because her senses were heightened in the shifted state and distracted her. Vague memories of Michelle, her parents, and her work with the horses, were becoming distant and difficult to grasp. A mourning emptiness filled her, and she searched down the mountain and whined, knowing it was Aaron's scent she missed.

For three days she traveled the ridgeline and cliffs and saw only grazing animals. She drank from streams and found berries and nuts that did not taste right, but she knew she must eat. Several times she looked around. Her deep indigo eyes were shot with steel gray, a reversal of their appearance when she was in her human form. Her gaze hunted through the rocks and sparse trees, and she had a feeling as though she was being watched. Lifting her muzzle and inhaling the smell of her surroundings, no one was ever there… at least, no one she could scent or see.

The remaining clan of Little People followed her journey, keeping her safe from bears and harm. Whether or not the girl should have been taken from the mountain to the flatlands, did not matter to them. They dealt only in the reality of now, and their visions had shown them that this cheéte and her friendship with the iishbíia would help close the protective circle for the iichíile.

They sensed her pain and uncertain desire to remain cheéte, and they admired her sacrifice. The Little People heard through the Crow shaman, of Nicholas' ambition and disregard for the herd. The spiritual ancients knew much more than that. The mystical dwarves had seen the cheéte round up prime feral stallions and sell them as breeding stock to ranchers wanting to take advantage of the sturdy mustang bloodline.

Through dreams, the Little People sent visions to rescuing wolves and cougars on the plains. They learned of the stallions' fate, and they managed to recapture most of the stolen horses. They were returned to the Baáhpuuo and their harems of mares and their foals were safely hidden in the mountains.

If this young wolf-girl could not fight through Nicholas' greed, there was little hope the cheéte and the iishbíia could survive, and without their protection, the beauty of the wild mustang would become extinct. They needed these magical shifter allies to fight for their land and search to find those auctioned and mistreated horses. To have a leader of the cheéte such as Nicholas working against the effort meant certain failure.

Lexi came to a little cave and she curled inside to rest. Her paws were raw from her journey and her muscles strained. After so long in wolf-form, she was learning to be comfortable and meld her spirits together. The Little People knew it was dangerous for her to remain in shifted-form for too much longer. Her human side would succumb, and slowly move aside to enjoy the freedom of her wild nature.

Lexi woke up to a bright morning sun. She stretched and laughed at her impossible predicament, realizing she was no longer a wolf. Yet, here she was, lost high in the mountains where she could not possibly survive in human form. When she sat up, she found a leather shift and moccasins placed by the entrance to the cave. Inhaling, she scented no one and slowly dressed. This seemed like just another crazy side-track which couldn't hold a candle to the thought she had just spent three days as a wolf.

"Well, whoever you are, thank you," she called through the entrance of the cave. Lexi's mind returned to more human thoughts. She wondered if Nicholas would go so far as to turn the shifters into the authorities. He could probably arrange it and remain unscathed, if he was willing to kill her mother. *Could I cower to his demands to keep them all safe?* An immediate ache gripped her heart and she saw Aaron, his bright blue eyes smiling and offering her safety and warmth.

"Mom sacrificed," she murmured.

"But, only to keep you from Nicholas," a man replied.

She spun around to see an Indian standing by her cave. Lexi's fists clenched and loosened while she stared at him. She looked down at her clothes. "Did you bring me these?"

He nodded and a smile creased his features. "It is not wise to spend too much time as cheéte." The Indian looked at the sky. He understood well the lure of the beast. "There are times I wish I could fly forever." He wandered behind her in silence for a long while. "Do you know what you must do?"

Lexi shook her head. "All I've ever wanted was my home with my father. Now, everything is mixed up."

"Come, cheéte. Follow me."

Lexi trailed behind him to a ridge overlooking a valley. She froze and gazed out on the green mountain grasses and tears filled her eyes. "They're beautiful," she whispered in awe.

Grazing in different parts of the valley, mustangs grouped in harems with mares playing sentry and guarding the herd. Stallions battled impressively, rearing and pawing, biting and ramming until a defeated opponent wandered off. Foals pranced and jumped around their herd, or dipped their heads beneath their mothers to nurse.

A group began running and other herds joined the stampede, thundering across the valley and kicking up dust, before settling down again to graze. These were

Spanish mustangs, with narrow chests and gorgeous colors.

The Indian looked down and smiled at her tears while she rubbed her heart. "You feel their spirit and pride within you."

Lexi continued to gaze out at them. "I always have."

The Indian placed a strong hand on her shoulder. "You will make the right decision, cheéte."

"How? I can't fight Nicholas, and if I join with him, he becomes leader."

The Indian gazed into her eyes, and he smiled. "You have something he doesn't. You have the iishbíia and Crow on your side."

Instinctively, Lexi understood the Indian name for the wolf and cougar. "I thought they got along. Brent is Nicholas' friend."

"Brent was Nicholas' guard," the Indian stated flatly. "Though, Paul has already extended welcome to your father and Aaron." He shrugged and kicked his moccasin through the grass. "It was a stupid argument, anyway."

"Why were the cougars and wolves fighting?"

"Silas sees no room in the circle for the iishbíia, and I think Nicholas would just as soon try to cut the wolf ties with the Crow." The Indian shook his head. "How does he expect to keep the circle, with only the wolves banded together?" After a few more moments of watching the horses, he added, "I suspect Nicholas had something to do with increasing the argument."

The Indian continued to gaze over the herd, smiling at a flashback memory of his ancestors riding the proud horses into battle. Wistful longing filled him, and he forced himself to shake free from the vision. It had been many seasons since he had kicked his father's stallion and had wandered to the Baáhpuuoto. When he travelled back to his village he had not only returned to his tribe a strong man, for the Little People had given the young boy a part of their magic in return for his promise to protect the circle. He alone held the secret to heal the cheéte and iishbíia, and he had remained a shaman with his tribe long after the Apsaalooke became known as Crow.

He studied the she-wolf watching the mustangs with her fist clenched over her heart. Perhaps it was a good thing she had not been raised among the turmoil that had infiltrated the shifters. "Angela was Paul's daughter, and her intended mate was to be the new leader of the iishbíia. They were not yet bonded when he was found slashed and bitten on the mountain. Angela already had their baby growing inside of her, and she left the mountain to hide her shame and to keep the child safe from the murderer." He smiled with compassion. "Your friend is pureblood cougar, and through her the leader's bloodline is brought back to the Baáhpuuoto."

Lexi was silent for a moment, envisioning the sight of the torn cougar who had been Michelle's father and comparing that to the scene of Jacob, covered in blood on the ranch floor. She turned to look up at him. "Nicholas would have been too young."

The shaman watched her closely. He stood straighter, gathering both his own inner memories and whirling clouds over their heads. The magic of the Baáhpuuoto built within him, and he focused his knowledge of the past into the girl. Suddenly, Lexi dropped to her knees, overwhelmed as her mind became completely filled with a vision of Silas and Nicolas. She heard their voices, felt their terrible thoughts, and she saw through their eyes.

"Just do it, Nicholas." The sun had risen an hour ago, and Silas was anxious to get this business done with. He and

his son stood still in the thick brush at the edge of the foothills, staring down on the valley below them. A white stallion grazed silently with his herd of three mares and the two foals born last fall. The thought of the money the stallion would bring was the enticing lure bringing them to the mountain, but Silas was immediately distracted by the she-wolf guarding the perimeter. Now, it was this beast he watched closely.

Nicholas fixed his sight on the wolf, and then he lowered the barrel of the gun. "I'm only going to wing her," he whispered to his father. "It won't do me any good to kill her, before I find out where she's hidden her daughter." He lifted the barrel of his gun again, and trained it on the she-wolf.

Silas watched the scene unfolding, and he felt no sense of guilt issuing the order. His son still had a lot to prove to him, before Silas felt he was ready to lead the pack. Nicholas had the ambition. He certainly wasn't the sappy weakling his twin turned out to be, but sometimes his judgment seemed off. A few times, Silas caught Nicholas barreling into fights and already attempting to usurp his father's authority. He decided a tighter rein on his son would help.

Silas knew Nicholas was consumed with thoughts of claiming his mate. The instinctive, yearning feelings building inside his son would make it impossible for Silas to fight Nicholas' goal to have his mate return to the mountain... along with her father. Jacob. Just thinking about the man pissed Silas off. Chances were, Jacob would not be able to reclaim leadership of the pack after being gone from the mountains for so long. Nicholas focus was on the girl though, and he was not considering the problems Jacob could cause his father when he returned.

Silas stared at the she-wolf lying in the grass and watching the horses. Vanessa's presence was a constant reminder that he had risen to pack leader by default. By all rights, it was her mate who should hold the position. Unfortunately, the small she-wolf remained with the pack; a clouded threat that Silas' leadership could be challenged if her husband ever returned. However, killing her would ensure Jacob would not challenge for the position. Silas relished the thought that Jacob would be despondent and spiral into despair with news of Vanessa's death.

But would he? Jacob had successfully managed to live away from his wife for fifteen years under the guise of protecting their daughter. Shit, from what? Nicholas? The girl should count herself lucky to have such a strong, alpha mate.

Silas held back his anger and continued to watch Vanessa. It was rare to find the she-wolf alone and not in the company of his youngest son, Aaron. When Silas had seen her guarding the herd, an anxious desire hit him. A desire even greater that capturing the stallion. He wanted the she-wolf dead and the threat to his position gone. After considering the situation, Silas reluctantly decided his son was right. They needed Vanessa alive, to divulge her daughter's location. Even if it meant Jacob would return with the girl to the mountain, they had to ensure she was mated to Nicholas. "Are you sure Vanessa hasn't told Aaron?"

Nicholas inhaled a deep, exasperated breath. "If my twin knew where our mate was, he would have gone to Jacob to plead his case," he replied irritably. "No, Vanessa doesn't trust Aaron, either."

Silas shook his head keeping predatory, icy blue eyes fixed on the she-wolf. Vanessa was still lying in the grass, but her head was raised and she was scenting the air. They were downwind from her, so Silas was fairly certain their presence was still hidden from her. He was not as certain that his youngest son had not learned where Jacob had taken the girl.

Aaron seemed to have formed a close relationship with Vanessa, and there was a better chance he had only decided to respect her wishes and not look for her daughter. After all, Aaron would only torture himself further with the knowledge that even if he did search the girl out, she belonged to his brother. As much as Silas acknowledged Nicholas' inherent urges to claim his mate, he disregarded that these same feelings consumed Aaron.

Silas scanned the grasses and low hills at the sides of the valley, and he could not see any sign of his youngest son. His nostrils flared and Silas thought he detected Aaron's scent wafting down from higher cliffs. The last thing he wanted was to be caught capturing the stallion, either by Aaron or Vanessa. *And if either one of them discovered it was Nicholas who shot the she-wolf, and not some white hunters trespassing on their lands... no, we won't be seen. Vanessa had not even turned her head in their direction.*

Silas knew Aaron's affection for the woman. He would panic and ignore everything else when he saw Vanessa lying shot in the pasture. Hurting her would be the distraction they needed, and he growled at Nicholas, "Shoot her, dammit."

They had carefully planned the capture, deciding where they needed to stand so that when the shot rang out the horses would bolt forward. At the sound of the shotgun, they would run directly into the makeshift corral that funneled to the entrance to Wooten's Trail. Silas and Nicholas would have plenty of time to close the rail gate and keep the horses contained, and they could easily cull the stallion from the small herd. Then, it was merely getting it loaded into the waiting trailer, remove the pipe railing, and leave no sign of their trap.

"What if my brother…"

"Aaron is hunting in the cliffs. When he hears the shot, he'll scamper down to the valley and find Vanessa. He'll be busy helping her and ignore the horses. The distraction will give us plenty of time to collect the stallion and release the rest of the herd." Silas was getting impatient, and he kicked Nicholas' shin. "You aren't backing out on me, are you boy?"

Nicholas growled in reply and lifted the shotgun to his shoulder. The loud report was answered by the shrieking wail of the she-wolf and the sound of galloping horses. The bullet was meant to sideswipe Vanessa's leg, but at the last second she had lifted her head and stared in their direction, scenting the air and taking a step forward. The bullet lodged deep into her thigh, and she scanned the hills in shocked confusion before rolling onto the grass. Her wolf howls disintegrated *into those of a sobbing woman, screaming for Aaron to help her.*

Silas' stared, fascinated by the sight of the injured woman and inhaling the copper smell of blood in the breeze. Nicholas was already moving towards the entrance to the trail, but Silas remained transfixed as his mind flashed back to a similar scene two decades ago. It was a time before Vanessa gave birth to her daughter, and five years before her mate would take the child and disappear from the mountains.

Nicholas and Aaron, his twins, were barely old enough to walk. They remained at the caves with their mother while Silas hunted. At least, that was what he was supposed to be doing. Instead, Silas had begun secretly capturing prime stallion stock and selling the mustangs to southern ranches to breed the superior blood into their herds.

After two successful transactions, a young cougar caught onto to Silas' activities. Silas suggested the cat join up with him, but the cougar merely gave him a sad look and turned to report him to the elders and Crow mediator. He had left Silas no choice, but instead of a gun Silas shifted and he tore the cougar to pieces.

Carefully clawing open the wounds, he made it appear that a bear had killed the cat. Silas shifted back to a man and as he kicked the cougar's corpse, he looked up into the terrified, anguished green eyes of Angela. Silas aimed his gun at her, and she gripped her stomach and ran. He knew there was only one reason she would not have attacked the wolf that had killed her mate. Angela was protecting a baby. Silas smiled, and the gaze from his icy blue eyes followed the panicked cougar as she scampered down the mountain. There was nothing she could do for her mate, and Silas knew that her fear for her child would keep her lips sealed.

By the time Silas had returned from selling the stallion he had captured, Angela had left her pack and run to the flatlands to hide. It was several days before her mate was discovered, and Silas joined the others to search for the rogue bear that had killed him.

Paul was already leader of the cougars, by then. He grieved not only for the loss of their future pack leader, but for his beautiful daughter. The thought that she ran from the support of the pack upset him so badly, he sent word through shifters on the plains to find her.

Despite their efforts, Angela remained hidden. She managed to hang onto a thread of sanity long enough to give birth to her baby. Even the sight of the green-eyed kitten could not ease her pain, and within a few months Angela died of despair from the loss of her mate. She had never told her pack she was pregnant. Silas knew, but there was no way he could tell the cougars without divulging his culpability in the tragedy. He allowed one of the shifters greatest rules to be broken, and let Angela's baby be placed in adoption.

Silas heaved a heavy sigh and began to follow Nicholas' tracks. A jolt of nervousness hit him, as Silas considered how many of his sins had stacked up over the years. He had murdered the cougar, let a shifter child be placed in a regular flatland home, and now, he had brought his eldest son into his deceitful business. Perhaps, this would be his greatest sin, for he had broken the circle of protection surrounding the mustangs.

"Well, shit," Silas muttered, as he followed Nicholas' trail through the brush to their makeshift corral. He had been selling the mustangs for twenty years, and even helped the BLM by convincing the shifters and Crow to pass an auction a few years ago. As nothing bad had happened, Silas decided the Crow legends about the Little People were just stories to keep their lands protected by the shifters. The Indians followed their eccentric shaman's beliefs in a lot of weird mojo fantasies.

In the valley, Vanessa was certain she caught Nicholas' scent just before a bullet ripped through her thigh. She silently begged the horses to run up to the cliffs, and she watched helplessly as they galloped towards the entrance to Wooten's Trail. Sobbing, she clutched her leg and tried to stem the flow of blood seeping through her fingers. "Aaron...

Aaron, please." Her fingers were shaking and she could feel the blood pouring out of her body. The bullet had torn a jagged rip in the vein, and even her ability to heal rapidly could not mend the tear while the bullet was still lodged inside of her.

By the time Aaron found her, the herd had returned to nervously grazing in the valley... minus the white stallion. He shifted as he ran to her, glancing briefly at the foothills and scenting for signs of the hunters. Aaron knew he would have to search for them later. He needed to take care of Vanessa, first.

"Take me to the caves," Vanessa cried.

Aaron lifted her, and he could already feel the weakness in the arms slung over his shoulders. "You need the Crow shaman." He tried to figure out where Silas would be. All requests to the Indians had to pass through the pack leader, first. Vanessa was losing blood so fast, Aaron wasn't sure there would be enough time.

"No. Just bring me home, please," she begged.

"Vanessa..."

"No, Aaron, please. You can help me. I don't want to bother Silas or the Crow. I think if you get the bullet out, I can heal."

Aaron ran with her in his arms, bypassing the trail and taking the shortcut up through the cliffs. Vanessa was limp and practically unconscious by the time he laid her on the blankets of her cave. He managed to remove the bullet and finally stopped the bleeding. For the next few days, he nursed her through fevers. Aaron listened to her rant for Jacob to keep Lexi safe. By now, he was aware that Vanessa's daughter, the girl who would have been his mate, was destined to belong to his older brother. Aaron knew Vanessa disliked Nicholas, and in her delirium she was blaming him for the hunting accident.

Paul, the cougar leader, brought him some medicine. He urged Aaron to let him talk to Silas and summon the Crow shaman, but Vanessa kept pleading for them not to. Aaron applied the antibiotic to the wound, but it still festered for almost a month. It wasn't healing right, and Aaron could scent a slow moving poison had leached into her bloodstream. No matter how much he tried to convince her, every attempt to let him report the incident to Silas and get the healer was squelched with her pleading tears.

Because of Aaron's kindness, Vanessa was determined not to let him know that his twin brother had been the one who had shot her. Her glimpse through the brush had shown her that Silas had been with him, and Vanessa shivered at the thought her daughter, Lexi, was to belong to Nicholas.

220

Obviously, there was no way she could let Aaron go to his father.

When Vanessa had recovered enough for Aaron to take short trips from the cave, the cougars joined with him to search for signs of the man who had shot her. Hunters rarely trespassed on their land, but the pungent smell they left behind from laundered clothes, tobacco, liquor and such, usually made them easy to trace. With more than a week passing since the incident and several rains, the only scents they could pick up were those of other shifters. Any human scent of the hunters had been washed away.

It was another two months, before Silas travelled to their caves. Vanessa was sitting by the fire, and Aaron felt queasy when his father did not seem alarmed to discover she had been shot. He didn't even inquire as to whether Aaron had managed to track the hunters responsible, and he dissuaded them from seeking the healer. Aaron wondered if Paul or one of the other cougars had told him. If so, why hadn't he visited earlier and demanded justice for the attack? Instead, his father began pressing Vanessa for information about her daughter.

"Vanessa, it's not right to keep Nicholas' mate from him. Do you want to be responsible for the future leader of your pack falling into despondency? Possibly descending into a permanent shift and remaining a wolf to escape his despair?

And what of your daughter?" Silas was relieved when he noticed her finally reacting, and the she-wolf's eyes sparkled indigo throughout the gray.*

Silas persisted with his manipulative attack. "She belongs here, Vanessa. Back with her own kind." He placed a hand on hers. "How long has it been since you've seen your own mate? Jacob should be taking care of you, not my son."*

"I don't mind," Aaron interjected. He sat on Vanessa's other side and took her hand out from under his father's. She was trembling and Aaron squeezed her hand gently.*

"Aaron," Vanessa said softly, "what will happen if Lexi shifts away from the mountains and is confused because she can't find her mate?"*

Aaron shrugged miserably. "Jacob will explain it to her, Vanessa."*

Silas glared at him. "I see. Because you had the misfortune of being born second cub, you will deny your brother his mate? He is your pack leader, Aaron," Silas reminded him.*

"Nicholas is not pack leader, yet. If Vanessa wants Lexi to remain on the..."*

"Vanessa has been listening to your selfish ideas," Silas muttered. "It was a mistake to leave you here to mislead her." He returned his attention to Vanessa, and his eyes lightened to the threatening warning ice blue. "How can you justify running off your mate? You know damn well a pureblood can't survive off the mountain. It almost killed you."

Vanessa cringed against the assault of his accusations and she leaned against Aaron. Silas stood. "Nicholas shifted two years ago, Vanessa. It's a pretty good bet your daughter's already having the dreams. Remember them? Remember how they twisted your mind and insides until you came back to the mountain? Is that what you want for Lexi, Vanessa? Do you want your daughter to suffer with no idea how to stop them?" His scathing, verbal attack continued, and she wanted to cover her ears.

Vanessa began crying quietly. She was so very tired of speaking with Silas, and the questions he brought up had frightened her. Her heart ached with loneliness for her daughter and her mate, and Silas' suggestions that Lexi should have remained with the pack made sense. To have thrust this all on Jacob's shoulders, might have been unfair to both of them.

Jacob had written and alluded to the fact that he thought Lexi was beginning to have the dreams, pulling her back to *the Baáhpuuo. Were they being selfish by trying to protect her? Vanessa's mind flashed onto the terrible visions she had when she tried to leave the mountain to join Jacob and her daughter. She couldn't bear the thought of Lexi suffering such agony.*

Ultimately, Vanessa confessed her location to Silas. He shifted and let out a triumphant howl, while she sagged against Aaron, sobbing and praying to the Little People that she had done the right thing.

The Crow stared at Lexi intently, his dark brown eyes waiting patiently for her to respond. He saw the realization fill her eyes. The shaman watched her slowly return from her vision of the past while the clouds overhead parted and the sun shone down on them again.

"Silas? Oh my god. Do the cougars know?"

"They suspect, and it is why they no longer speak or get along. Nicholas comes by his ambition honestly, and as you now know, it was he who shot your mother. Silas, the twins' father, forgot his agreement to the Crow and the mustangs many years ago. He has not only allowed the iichíile to be auctioned and ignored the agreements we fought so hard to set in place, Silas and Nicholas capture stallions and sell them to places far from their home in the Baáhpuuoto. Silas has never felt or understood that the cougars are a necessary part of his ancestors' agreement to complete the circle of protection."

Lexi sighed. "It's all so complicated, and this still doesn't help me decide what to do."

The shaman stared at the fist she held clenched on her chest. "What is in your heart, cheéte?"

"To be with my family and friends," Lexi answered. Gazing across the field, she smiled. "And to protect the mustangs."

"That is your strength, then. Draw on this and feel their spirit."

Lexi continued to stare at the horses, and when she turned to speak to the Indian, he was gone. A screech of a bird called from overhead. It was a bird no white man had ever seen; the apsaalooke that had disappeared from the skies centuries ago. She watched it fly down to the valley, circle the horses, and fly towards the plain.

She looked around, and then called after the bird. "Hey, where the heck am I?" Lexi had no idea how to get back. "Well, shoot." She was pulled towards the mustangs and slowly made her way down to the valley.

The horses let her wander among them, occasionally lifting their heads to acknowledge her passing. Foals pranced around her, playfully whinnying and kicking up their heels. It was a very different, calm acceptance, than what she experienced with the captured mustangs she worked with. "Nicholas would have had no problem catching you," she said to a beautiful white stallion standing a few feet away and staring at her.

The horse snorted and continued gazing at her. Deep within his spirit, far back to the time of his ancestors, the horse envisioned a small Indian boy searching for his own true spirit. It was one of his iichíile ancestors that had sent the Crow boy into the Baáhpuuo, and the same uncertain pride filled the cheéte now wandering among them.

Lexi felt such a strong connection to the stallion, that the thought of the a stunning horse being taken from his home in the valley, lay heavy inside of her. She knew that she had to figure out a way to stop the captures, and she wandered back up to the cave.

Chapter XIII

Michelle's arm healed quickly. She spent her time with Brent, Sophia, and Paul who shared memories of her mother. He was truly happy to discover Michelle was his granddaughter and constantly spoke with pride at her courage to stand up to Nicholas. Paul was brokenhearted at the loss of his daughter. His mate had died many years ago, and he had no idea Angela was pregnant when he had found the note saying she was leaving for the flatlands. Paul had a sinking feeling why his daughter left. She must have known her mate was dead… perhaps, seen that it was not any fight with a bear… and she fled to keep her baby safe.

The confusion and conflict with the wolves kept Paul busy, and Michelle focused most of her time getting to know her mate and learning what it meant to be iishbíia. A few times she ran with him in cougar form, up the mountain to sit with Vanessa and wait for Lexi's return. Jacob was with her, taking over Aaron's duties of caring for his mate.

Aaron spent two days trying to catch Lexi's scent up the mountain. He had come to the sad conclusion it had been masked somehow, and there was no sign of her paw prints or broken limbs marking her passage. Reluctantly, he returned to the others and guarded the clearing, wanting Lexi to return and afraid of Nicholas' reaction when she did.

Nicholas spent time at the ranch with Silas, predictably scheming for control and leadership of the wolves. Lexi was gone and presumably dead with her inadequate ability for life alone on the mountain. The two wolves were planning to announce that with Silas the accepted leader, his eldest son should be the natural choice to replace him.

When Michelle and Brent returned to Sophia's house on the plains, Aaron finally approached Jacob and Vanessa and he told them what he knew of Angela's mate's death. It incriminated both Silas and his brother, as Aaron admitted the cougar had been killed to keep the cougars from having a leader. In return, Vanessa reluctantly admitted that it had been Nicholas and Silas wandering through the brush when she had been shot. She argued until she collapsed in exhaustion, to keep Aaron and Jacob from going after them. They finally agreed to wait, rather than risk her health.

"Paul should be told," Jacob said. "And the Indians. They have a right to know for their years of protecting the circle."

"Concerning Angela's mate, I think everybody suspects what happened already," Aaron admitted. "It's just something that is never discussed." Aaron swirled a stick on the ground. "What will happen if the cougars and Crow find out the wolves sold the horses and have gone so far as to hurt the shifters to protect their secret?"

Jacob shrugged. "Don't know, boy. Maybe we lose the power to shift… maybe nothing. Be ironic if after all Silas' planning, all that was left were the cats up here."

It was another few days before the group in the clearing was startled by the sound of pounding hooves running up the trail. Michelle jumped up and held Brent's hand, and her face broke into a smile when Lexi rode into the space on the back of a beautiful white mustang. The stallion rose on his hind legs, snorting and whinnying while Lexi clung to his mane. There were three mares and an excited dancing foal, kicking up his heels and snorting bravely with the game.

Lexi stroked the horse's neck and stared deep into his eyes. He threw his head and looked at his harem, before galloping down to the plain. It would be a while before he returned to the valley and alerted the herd it was once more safe to travel to the lower rolling hills.

No one said a word about her Indian clothes, and Lexi ran up to give her parents a hug. She took Aaron's hand, but she looked at Michelle. "We've got work to do."

Sitting around the fire, she asked Jacob, "Tell me about the men who shot grandpa." It was a different set of laws and rules in the hills, and outsiders could not help them. She knew turning Silas and Nicholas into authorities for the murder or for selling the mustangs, could mean the demise of everything.

Jacob's eyes narrowed on her. "You aren't thinking about shooting them, are you Lexi? We don't' do that to our own."

"Well, Dad, I wouldn't blame the cougars for tearing into Silas, but it's obvious that isn't how Paul wants to handle it or he would have acted by now. And Nicholas will have to pay for what he's done to Mom and you." She gazed up into the mountains. "I have something else in mind, but it means leaving again."

Aaron said, "I'm coming with you."

"Good. I want Michelle and Brent to come with us, too."

"Lexi, what are you thinking, girl?" There was uncertain warning in Jacob's tone.

"I'm saving the mustangs, Dad." A bird in the tree cawed in approval and Lexi found it sitting high on a branch. She called up, "Hey, don't run out on me again. I need you to show me the way back to the cave."

The group argued the best way to handle things, and in the end, Vanessa insisted on joining them. She took her daughter aside. "Lexi, I might not make it another winter, and it's partly Nicholas' fault I've missed all this time with you. I deserve to see justice for those lost years." She ran a thin hand down her daughter's hair. "You won't be able to go back down to the flatlands, you know. Your bloodline and pull to the Baáhpuuo is much too strong."

Lexi looked over at Aaron and she smiled. There was no way she could possibly leave him, or expect him to make the sacrifice of moving from the mountains. "I know, Mom. What about Michelle?"

"She's planning on telling her parents she wants to finish her degree out here. She figures she can do it online at Sophia's house. We'll just have to be careful when her parents visit, but we're all used to that."

"What about Sunchaser Ranch?"

Vanessa looked over at Jacob. "Your father might return for a while." She saw the concern in her daughter's eyes and she gave her a weak hug. "Don't worry so much, Lexi. Jacob knows how to take care of himself. Except for the coffee," she added. "Your father and I will begin walking up the mountain tonight. Give us a couple days head start and we'll meet you."

"You know where the cave is?"

"Lexi, I've been running through the hills chasing ghosts for fifteen years. I know the spot near the valley of the horses. I loved to run with them and be free from my loss for a while, when I was stronger."

After dinner, Vanessa and Jacob shifted. It was still half an hour before Vanessa was strong enough to begin the slow walk up the mountain. Lexi watched her father nuzzle branches out of the way and clear a path for his mate. "I feel so guilty for keeping them apart," Lexi said.

Aaron put his arm around her. "This was their decision, Lexi. I think Vanessa always knew my brother would try to claim you. He was not much better when he was younger." He stood and held his hand down to her. "They are together now, and that's how it should be. If you ask them, even with the way things turned out, they would not have done things differently."

Lexi pulled herself up beside him, and she turned to search once up the path, flaring her nostrils and smelling her parents' scent, before letting Aaron lead her to his cave.

From the light of the fire flickering across the stone walls, Lexi looked up at him. She came up to his broad shoulders, and she combed her fingers through his long dark hair while his gray-blue eyes gazed down at her.

Just as in her dreams, Lexi saw blankets were laid on the dirt floor, and she smiled up into Aaron's shadowed face. She felt none of the fear or sense of loss she had in her visions. There was only the promising comfort of the man embracing her.

Aaron pulled her close against the warmth of his chest, and he murmured, "This is where you're meant to be." He leaned down, and Lexi felt a thrill course through her when he kissed her.

Aaron guided them down onto the blankets and caressed her cheek with his thumb. "I didn't know you would be so beautiful," he murmured.

Lexi smiled. "I sorta' wondered when I'd hear you say that." She laughed at the confusion on his face, and threw her arms around his neck and kissed him again.

* * * *

Michelle and Brent stayed down on the plains, discussing Lexi's return with Sophia and Paul. The two older cougars had become close since Michelle's return to the mountain, and they were forming a comfortable friendship. Paul kept Nicholas and Silas busy, until it was time to initiate Lexi's plan.

It was finally time for Aaron and Lexi to travel down Wooten's Trail and face the two wolves. "Are you certain?"

"It's the only way, Aaron. At least we're giving them a choice."

They shifted and ran down the path, stopping by a shack hidden in the trees behind the sign to Wooten's Trail. Inside was a mish-mash of odd colored clothes in various sizes. Aaron grinned while he gazed at her.

Lexi was already more comfortable in wolf-form and rarely blushed between changes.

They walked to the ranch and saw Nicholas sitting on the porch. He jumped up and called something back into the house, and Silas walked out and joined him. Nicholas glared at his brother. "You can't have her," he stated. His hair bristled on the back of his neck in outrage, seeing that his mate lived and that she was so happy standing beside Aaron.

"I have a proposition, Nicholas," Lexi countered.

"You aren't in a position to bargain," he snapped.

Lexi ignored Nicholas, and she turned to the leader standing silently beside him. "Silas, what happened to Angela's mate?"

Before Silas could answer, Michelle came around the side of the house with Brent, Paul, and Sophia. "Yes, Silas. What happened to my father?"

Silas took a step back towards the door. "How the hell should I know?" he growled. "The damn cat went hunting and caught up with a bear, I was told."

"Pretty damn convenient, leaving my daughter without a mate to claim blood lineage to leader. It would make it rather easy for the wolves to takeover," Paul suggested. "You knew you had Vanessa's daughter, and Angela would have none, leaving no leader for the cougars."

Silas nodded towards Michelle. "She's here, isn't she?"

"Don't think we haven't traced who demanded proof of her pureblood, Silas. You figured she was a half-breed," Brent stated.

Silas had not been all that surprised, as he had suspected the cougar was pregnant when she took off after he'd killed her mate. "Well, she's all cat. You must be proud," Silas sneered.

Lexi was a bit confused about the hatred in his voice, and then it dawned on her. "He caught you."

"Caught what? You're a flatlander. You don't know what the hell you're talking about. When Nicholas gets you under control…"

"Angela's mate caught you selling the mustangs." She looked at Nicholas. "Did you catch Silas too? Or did you just decide to join him on your own?"

Nicholas' eye twitched. *How can anyone know about that? The mustangs are at private ranches in Nevada.* "What are you accusing me of?"

"Where are all the iichíile, Nicholas? There should be more than the herds I've seen on the foothills and up in the valley."

"Who knows?" he snarled. "Who cares? We're fighting BLM to keep them from auctioning them, because they're tearing up the cattle's grazing land and busting down the fences. Half the time, we find them wandering in the state forest and the cats don't do a damn thing to control them."

"We care, because we have agreed to protect them. Luckily, rescue groups on the flatlands have upheld that commitment and returned the horses you stole."

"I don't know what you're talking about."

"Don't you? Or have your friends not bothered to call when the rescuers cart them away." Lexi turned and looked up at the mountains. "I found them, Nicholas. And our people, who collected them and brought them back, know the truth about what you did."

Silas smiled. "And what do you intend to with this information? The same society and authorities we hide from, is a society you can't turn us into. The Crow sure as blazes aren't going to get involved."

Lexi smiled at him. "I'm referring to the mystics who charged us with protecting the circle, Silas. The Little People of the Baáhpuuo."

Silas and Nicholas stared at each other, and then they turned back to Lexi and burst out laughing. "You wandered too long in those mountains, girl. Got yourself dazed," Silas smirked.

"Then, you won't mind going up there."

"You want us to trek through the Pryor Mountains, looking for the seven dwarves?" Silas shook his head.

Nicholas stared at her, his mind spinning. She wasn't really one of them, and she might do something stupid that could expose them. "Okay, let's say we go up for a few days. If we don't find these Little People, what then? You still can't turn us into authorities."

"No, that's true. But, I think between two wolves and three cougars, not everyone would come out alive."

"You'll kill us?"

Lexi shrugged. "Only if you don't agree. If we go up, and we don't find the Little People, I'll stay with you. That makes you leader, Nicholas." She had to really argue this agreement with Aaron, considering she had never actually seen the Little People when she journeyed up there.

"And you leave us alone about thinning the herd?"

"It won't come to that," she replied confidently.

Ultimately, Nicholas and Silas decided it was better to go along with her delusion. This was just another Crow legend made up to explain things they couldn't understand. It would be easier to continue their operation, with Nicholas as leader. The first thing he intended to do was put the cougars back in place.

It took them two days, as the 'Crow' flies, to reach the cave. Vanessa looked worn from the trip, but pleased to be included.

Nicholas glared at the happy couple, and then he looked back at Lexi. He couldn't wait to tame the irritating she-wolf. "What now?" Nicholas asked. "Do we need some mumbo jumbo words to chant before you realize how stupid this is?"

"That won't be necessary." The group turned and while some gasped, Lexi and Michelle smiled down at the five diminutive men. The Indian stood beside them, running his fingers down the length of his knife, obviously prepared to fight to the death to protect them. As a boy, there had been nine of the Little People. The ancient leader remained, watching the others take their final journey.

Silas turned sickly white, and Nicholas' eyes strobed between confusion and anger. "You tricked us," he snarled at Lexi.

"No, I told you they would be here. And you both agreed to abide by their judgment."

"If we knew they were real..." Silas whined helplessly, and the group realized he had been hiding his cowardice behind an arrogant façade.

"You don't need to see and feel something to believe in your spirit that it is right," Lexi replied. "They gifted us with the spirit of the wolf and cougar, in exchange for protecting the mustangs." The indigo in her eyes flashed. "You reneged on your agreement."

The men shuffled their feet uneasily. The big bad Indian mojo of the Baáhpuuo was about to slam them, and they knew they had no defense. "So, we won't do it again," Nicholas replied in a voice edged with panic.

"It is too late for that, cheéte," the little man said. "You split apart harems, leaving foals unprotected except for their mares. And worse, we were too late to save a young stallion from slaughter. An iishbíia was murdered on the Nevada plains, trying to save him. This one honorable duty you were prescribed, to make up for the heinous acts of your ancestors. This was the agreement to let your kind survive, for entering our mountains." The little man turned to the others and they nodded in agreement.

"They're horses. Just wild horses," Silas stuttered.

"And *you* broke the circle by killing the iishbíia," the ancient replied.

Silas cringed and he felt Nicholas raging beside him. *He's trying to shift*, Silas realized. He reached for his own center, willing the form of the wolf and intent on tearing the group apart… beginning with the little monsters. At first he panicked, unable to feel the sharp quick blackout overtake him. At last it flashed through his mind, and he smiled in triumph while he and Nicholas changed.

Epilogue

Vanessa's soft voice called out, "Lexi, it's time to load up."

She smiled over at her mother. The Little People had done Lexi another favor, and granted Vanessa her health. "Hold on, Mom." She smiled at the squealing babies on the grass and laughed. "Honestly, Aaron, you're worse than trying to get Dylan ready."

"Brent." Michelle stood, rolling her eyes and picking up Hannah as she crawled over her cougar daddy's soft fur. "Shift and get dressed. It's time to leave."

Lexi tugged at the wolf's ear. "Get a move on, Aaron. Dad's been ready for ten minutes." The wolf nipped at her fingers and she laughed again, causing the baby to roll into peals of laughter. They could play together like this for a few more years, and then the secret of their heritage would have to be guarded until their children were older.

Vanessa joined Jacob in the diesel, pulling the Sunchaser horse trailer. Lexi and Michelle followed them, with their families loaded into a van. Paul and Sophia made up the rear of the caravan, towing another horse trailer.

This was the first sanctioned auction of Pryor Mountain mustangs held in many years. The rescue league had already checked the buyers, and was prepared to outbid anyone questionable. The sale had been discussed at length with the Crow, and it was agreed the sacrifice would have to be made to appease their agreement with the BLM.

When they drove into the dusty dirt lot of the Wyoming auction site, they backed the trailers to the gate and led the horses into a round-pen. A chute was on one side of the fence, and an experienced wrangler was prepared to freeze brand the cryptic BLM code on the left side of the mustangs' necks. It would distinguish which territory the mustangs came from, their age, and their registered number.

Lexi walked up to a bay stallion and the horse tried to bite her. "Oh come now, Nicholas." He had an angry look in his eyes, with more than a bit of confusion. Lexi could sense that his human spirit was sinking beneath that of the mustang, and she decided this was not such a bad thing.

She glanced over at a furious gray with a shaggy white mane, pawing the dirt. Silas fought to keep his human side, and wore himself down with his futile attempts to shift back. Lexi said quietly, "You didn't really think I'd let you and Nicholas off that easily, and have you spend your days frolicking in the mountains." The horse snorted at her. "You've earned this, Silas, and despite your treachery, the shifters will still look out for you."

Lexi liked the symmetry of the punishment. Nicholas and Silas could now spend their days as the mustangs they neglected. Even so, the shifter rescuers who had sacrificed the freedom of living on the Baáhpuuo to watch over the mustangs would diligently follow the path of the two shifted horses.

This was their purpose, and an honor celebrated when they returned to the mountains for the three day celebration in the summer. The iishbíia, cheéte, and Crow took that time each year to pay tribute to the Little People. In the two years Brent and Aaron held leadership over the shifters, the circle had become strong again.

Lexi and Michelle held their kitten and cub, standing together by the captured horses and trying to send them psychic messages of calmness. They had been carefully culled as those that could adapt to a domesticated life easier, and perhaps would enjoy the security a life of predicable care and feeding could provide.

Aaron and Brent held court with the shifter rescuers, answering questions and making decisions concerning new problems with BLM auctions in other areas. There were also a few special case horses that needed to be petitioned to be brought back to their life in the wild. The two men seemed to slip into the role of leaders easily, though they both spoke quietly about their dislike of the restraint of politics.

With his son sleeping in his arms, Aaron reached up to urge Dylan's little fist from his hair where the baby gripped through his father's dark waves. The little boy shuddered and relaxed when Aaron's strong hand stroked gently down his back. Never had he expected to feel such happiness. When he looked at his mate and his son, it made him shiver at the thought of how close he had come to remaining a wolf, traveling the cliffs and forests of the Baáhpuuo and howling his loneliness into the wind.

After the last horse was auctioned to an acceptable bidder, they drove back to the Pryor Mountains. There were stretches of silence as the shifters came to terms with the necessity of the day's activities. The BLM had been pressuring for more than a year to thin the Baáhpuuo herds. The horses were overgrazing the pastures and breaking down fences to move to the greener areas in the forest service park.

It was better to compromise and give them the mustangs that could adapt, then to risk a forced roundup every few years. Reluctantly, even the Crow agreed, but it did not sit well with any of them. The Indians and shifters would keep a vigilant eye on legislation that might be hidden in other Bills that could impact the mustangs.

The trucks and trailers passed under the Wolf Creek hanging sign, and Lexi felt the serene reassurance that she was home. After the babies were fed and sleeping, she and Michelle walked outside as another day came to an end.

Aaron followed Lexi's gaze towards the Baáhpuuo, and said, "Go ahead. Brent and I have things to discuss and we'll look after the kids." The men chuckled as the young women peeled off their clothes and ran towards the hills.

* * * *

A beautiful sunset spread a pastel wash over the valley, bursting light off jagged rock cliffs. A wolf and cougar lay on a grass hill looking down on the grazing wild horses. It was their twenty-third birthday, and they silently considered how their world had changed, yet strengthened their friendship.

Their paws rested over each other's, and the sun reflected off of two halves of a silver disk. On the chain around the wolf's neck dangled the profile of a cougar, while the cougar wore the friendship token in the shape of the wolf. A tattered princess crown sat in front of them on the grass, with the sun sparkling off the remaining patches of glitter.

The End

Screaming Mustangs

Mystic Mustangs - Book 2

Excerpt

"Lexi?"

Lexi balanced Dylan on one hip while she cradled the phone to her ear. His pudgy fingers reached for the coiled cord, and for the hundredth time she wished she had another cordless model. Unfortunately, her two year old son liked to find the handset wherever it was left, and he ran down the hall laughing while she scrambled after him. Twice the chase ended with the final kerplunk of the telephone's demise as it sunk to the bottom of the toilet. "Yes?"

"Lexi, this here's McMillan."

"Mac?" It had been months since she'd talked to her father's old friend from Florida. "How are you?" Lexi chuckled, and asked, "Better yet, how is Brutus?" She smiled with memories of the frustration his favorite horse caused him.

"He's fine. How's it going in the mountains?"

"We're all doing well. Mom and dad will be down to Sunchaser for the winter again. Montana's a bit rough on them." Luckily, Vanessa was no longer taunted by the dreams when she left the mountains for a few months.

"Look forward to seeing them both." There was silence for a moment, and then Mac said, "Look, I got a bit of a problem."

Lexi's senses peaked to alert, and she passed Dylan to Aaron as he walked by. "A mustang?" Her mind flew towards her list of rescuers in the area.

"No, nothing like that. Do you remember a couple years ago, you sold a pretty black gelding to a girl for barrels?"

Lexi knew immediately who he meant. She could still see the excitement in the young girl's eyes, with her red pigtails hanging under a blue cowboy hat. "Cindy Morrison. She lives with her grandfather."

"That's her." There was silence for a moment, again. "Look, Sam passed away. We got the rescue team to take care of the horses, but they hustled Cindy over to me before the authorities could get hold of her. They told people her mom came back for her, and so far, nobody's digging too deep."

"Good call on that one." Lexi chewed her bottom lip. "Guess it would be best to get her out of the area, before someone sees her on the circuit."

"Oh, she never took to the barrels. She rides Smokey for pleasure, but she took a liking to working with the mustangs," he chuckled.

"Yes, well we all know *that* story."

"Thing is, I can't keep her, Lexi. It's true someone might notice her, but I don't have any business trying to raise a fifteen year old girl, and the state will stick her in some kind of home."

"Then, I think it might be best to bring her back here. What do you have in mind?"

"Terry and Sarah Lipman are running a couple mustangs back to the mountain. BLM agrees they can't be tamed, and it's wearing the horses down being passed to different owners. I figure we can load Smokey and Cindy and let 'em tag along."

"She a wolf?"

"Cougar, though she don't know it yet."

"Send her out. I think Paul and Sophia can watch out for her until we can figure something else."

"Look for 'em in about two weeks, then. I'll pass your number along." Mac sighed. "Lexi, I think it's gonna' make it easier if I let Cindy know she'll be near you. She always looked up to you, and now she's got no one."

Lexi smiled. "Tell her I'm looking forward to riding with her, Mac. The poor girl has had a rough time of it."

After she hung up, Lexi called Sophia. She and Paul married a year ago. Sophia's mate died in a hunting accident when Brent was ten, and Paul's wife died many years ago. The couple shared a comfortable companionship, and although Brent was now cougar leader, Paul still liked to work on tracing bloodlines.

"Morrison, huh?" Paul rocked on Lexi's porch and squinted, staring into space. "Julia is her mom, and Cindy's father would be Tom."

"I guess her dad died in a car accident when she was ten. Julia tried to take care of her, and they ended up moving in with Sam. A year later, Julia took off and no one heard from her again," Lexi informed them.

"Damn." Paul shook his head. "We try to get them back to the mountains. Sometimes, even with a kitten or cub, they can't go on without their mate." Paul held Sophia's hand and he thought about his daughter, Angela. Even with a new baby, she could not survive without her mate. If she had not been so terrified of Silas, she might have returned to the mountains. Instead, the despair took hold of her, and she died before Paul could find her.

Lexi told them more about Cindy, and Paul shook his head, murmuring, "Poor kid."

Lexi stared over the porch railing towards the mountains. "I don't know, Paul. I've got a strange feeling about this. I think Julia is out there someplace."

"Well, we can certainly put the feelers out. If she is, she's going to be tied in with the mustangs," Sophia said. "And of course we'll take Cindy in. That's so much tragedy for such a little girl to bear."

* * * *

Nine hundred miles south of the Pryor Mountains and Lexi's ranch, silver spurs jangled as a wrangler walked towards a horse. The Nevada temperatures were already reaching down into the twenties at night, and the woman pulled the sheepskin collar up around her neck. She mounted her horse and headed towards the colorful foothills of the Calico Mountains at an easy lope.

It was early November and no one should be cruising the mustang protected lands, but from her small cabin, Julia Morrison had heard the rumble of truck engines two nights in a row.

It was dangerous, scouting out the slaughterhouse crew. They were willing to take chances for trucking the feral horses to Canada and Mexico for fistfuls of money. The men were ruthless. More so than the sly bidders sneaking into BLM auctions, and no one knew this better than Julia. She knew how far these cruel rustlers would go... far enough to stage the accident that killed her mate.

She stopped on a low hill overlooking a herd of grazing horses. The moon was full and she lay down on the grass, barely blinking while she tore at the jerky she pulled from her pocket. In the distance she heard a coyote cry, and it tugged deep inside of her. She had not shifted and run free as a cougar for years. It had been a silent promise to Tom, that she would not change form until it was time for his killers to pay. This was personal, and she intended to make every slashing swipe of her claws count.

She thought of her daughter, Cindy, safe with her grandpa and across the country from this horrible scene. It was far too dangerous to bring her back here, and Julia could not forget Tom and her need for vengeance long enough to be a proper mother to her. "Things will be better, baby," she whispered in the wind, only half believing it.

For years she had tracked the murderers, and now, she was close. So close she could smell the stink of the scent left on her dead husband's fur from the men. She tore at another strip of beef, chewing, gnashing… and imagining Luke and Jason Franklin's throats.

In the distance, Julia saw headlights bouncing across the frigid land below her. Her binoculars scanned the dimly lit ground and she located the small herd of mustangs, grazing quietly within a quickly constructed round pen. The rustlers had run the horses into the trap this morning, and Julia waited for the men to return to collect their prize.

Her gaze swept back to the approaching truck, and she sighed. The familiar, cramping dread gripped her stomach as she stood and quickly mounted her horse. She galloped towards the mustangs, waving her hat and whistling, while her spurs jangled in her stirrups.

Before the lights of the truck were around the last hill, the mustangs had broken through the enclosure and scattered. Julia had turned her mount and was well on her way back to her scouting place. Tears coursed down her cheeks and she dismounted again, staring helplessly at the pasture below her. The truck had stopped for a moment and began a slow turn.

The fugue state came over her and when Julia came to, the men had already collected the metal gates that had made up the enclosure and were traveling away from their trap. She had lost time again, and it frightened her. Weary and chilled, Julia climbed back on her horse for the ride back to her cabin.

After her horse was safe in the small barn, Julia walked into the drafty room that made up her home.

She stoked the fire to a warming blaze and pulled off her heavy coat. Julia knew she would spend another sleepless night, condemning herself for not letting the trapped mustangs remain captured long enough for her to complete her plan of vengeance for her mate.

Every time she got close, a painful clenching fear gripped her stomach, and she could not stop herself from saving the horses. At night when Julia closed her eyes, she had nightmares. She imagined a time when she followed through with her plan, and like her mate, she was killed. Because she had not scattered the horses, they weren't saved... and she woke to the sound of the mustangs' screams echoing in her mind as they were led to slaughter.